The Substitute Teacher

T0117072

Other Books by
Samson Kamura

Childhood Without a Mum in Africa

Its All Trouble

Blackman Too Hard For You

The Substitute Teacher

by
Samson Kamara

iUniverse, Inc.
New York   Bloomington

Copyright © 2009 by Samson Kamara

All rights reserved. No part of this book may be used or reproduced by any means, graphic, electronic, or mechanical, including photocopying, recording, taping or by any information storage retrieval system without the written permission of the publisher except in the case of brief quotations embodied in critical articles and reviews.

iUniverse books may be ordered through booksellers or by contacting:

iUniverse
1663 Liberty Drive
Bloomington, IN 47403
www.iuniverse.com
1-800-Authors (1-800-288-4677)

Because of the dynamic nature of the Internet, any Web addresses or links contained in this book may have changed since publication and may no longer be valid. The views expressed in this work are solely those of the author and do not necessarily reflect the views of the publisher, and the publisher hereby disclaims any responsibility for them.

ISBN: 978-1-4401-6645-7 (sc)
ISBN: 978-1-4401-6646-4 (ebook)

Printed in the United States of America

iUniverse rev. date: 08/18/2009

DEDICATED TO MY FATHER PA ALPHA KAMARA (RIP)

CHAPTER ONE

(INTRODUCTION)

TEACHING WAS A DETERMINED, dedicated and noble job when the teacher was appreciated and treated as a person with respect and dignity.

But being black and an immigrant from Black Africa was something totally different because from the lords of the manor, down the rank and file saw you as a black man, a foreigner, with an accent. Yak

The word substitute was interpreted literary by every one in the system from ordinary workers, to students, to school administrators and officials in the head office as untrained, unqualified, in experienced, and more or less a baby sitter in the classroom. This was because one was considered not a teacher, but a sit in person, irrespective of one's experience and qualifications.

As a substitute teacher, one was in the front line for discrimination at every level of a school department, by every one with a light skin color, and even non African black people would have negative attitudes towards the substitute if one was African. Yak

Even immigrants with similar status from other poor countries but with a light skin color would discriminate against the black African substitute especially if one was a substitute with no legal status and no say in every aspect of their job.

Looking at the system from top to bottom, there was a lot to be desired in the area of human relations which we believed had never been addressed.

It should be a hot topic for discussion in inner circles but a no go area.

The indication would be that the treatment of people of different races was, and would always be the same, a separate entity that would all the time be at the mercy of their presumed superiors the light skin colored.

And as one administrator in one ailing high school in the district of Yoni told Alpha one lunch time in the school cafeteria, that the system had not changed one iota of a point since he was employed some thirty years ago. He had worked in the system and everything was the same as it had always been all this time.

Changes were made in principle in administrative structures and personnel changed from time to time but the rubrics and the mechanics remained the same.

Who knew you was the order of the day as it was always the case. The teachers were frustrated, and disgusted with the politics of who was who which dominated the outlook.

The teachers became resigned to inactivity and lethargy, some teachers did not even teach at all either in protest or the feeling that nothing would ever changed and so why waste your time teach at all.

No wonder the state examinations told the whole story which no one took notice of except occasional noises, mud slinking and speaking behind closed doors

But being in the good books of the Senior Administrative officers of the institution and the district was all that mattered and not how hard you worked to survive in the system.

Even getting a job, getting regular teacher appointment and promotions in some school districts were based primarily on who knew you and your skin color.

One teacher told Alpha one day in the teachers' lounge that since he knew a man who was a friend of the principal and this man was doing odd jobs for the principal in his house. This handy man did odd jobs in his own house also, he mourned aloud in a casual conversation with the man about his status in the school. The handy man promised to press the button for him.

He was appointed as a regular teacher without any ceremony after this handy man told the principal to help the employment status of this neighbor.

The Principal simply told him that he had a job in the school from the next day.

But being black and African made it even worst, because not only the color, but the accent put you in a special category of disadvantaged people.

Alpha was a trained teacher with several years teaching experience, he had been substituting in the district for several years, but he could not make any head way.

People who came after him, with emergency certificates had been given regular jobs. Social studies and even English teachers had been given permanent positions to teach his subject in the high school, because of their favorite color and accent and the "who knew you" factor was in full swing.

It was off course natural that administrators always had preferences when it came to dealing with employees. A school district was no exception; and favorite teachers were very easy to pick out in a school community.

They knew the comings and goings in the school, the latest news, the pending events, where the administrator was, what the principal did each day. Gossip about other teachers and their standing within the school echelon, they knew when and where the Principal and senior administration were and where they would be each and every day.

Who knew you was a dominant factor, used to confirm positions, and promotions.

If you were black and a foreigner and you did not have a lobbyist on your side, you would surely be in the bottom of the pile and on the front line for terminations each year and you might never make it to a regular position. The pecking order in the Teachers Union contract was not worth the paper it was written on, as long as you were on the wrong side of the equation with your cultural capital and circumstances you were destined to stagnation.

Alpha had been kept behind as a substitute teacher with all his qualifications and experience because of his circumstances.

In the classroom too, it was not what you knew or what you could teach, the rule of thumb was keep the students in class each period everyday and do nothing, you would still be alright and in the good books of the officials.

This was supported by a statement from one veteran teacher in an ailing popular high school "These students were not meant to learn anything you only needed to keep them together for the class period. Nobody was going to ask you what you taught today and the students hardly complained and even if they did, nobody would listen or believed them or did anything about it."

Alpha had been in a school in the middle of the second quarter, and the class teacher before him had only covered two chapters in a thirty three chapter textbook meant for the class to cover in the school year. Some students note books had hardly more than four pages of class notes and exercises.

Students got "A" and "B" grades for good behavior in class and not for class work or academic excellence. As long as you behaved, did not ask silly questions or act silly in class and did as you were told, you were sure of a top grade at the end of the quarter and the label smart student.

It could be the reason why we were rated very low in International academic standing because most of the students called smart students had very good grades from the teachers but had very little if any knowledge of the subject

matter. Since a grade is all that mattered in the system and not what you knew or could remember.

It could also be the reason why some students in elite schools that supposedly accepted only gifted students did very poorly sometimes.

It could also be the most likely reason why Alpha was congratulated by the shortest lived head of department for having covered three chapters before he came over in the middle of the first quarter in the school year.

Mr. Bamba came over to Alpha's class for an introductory visit. He introduced himself as head of department but there was a negative reception from the big boys in the back seats.

Mr. Bamba tried to exert his authority as head of the department. One of the students was so nasty to him that Alpha had to talk to the student to calm down. Mr. Bamba took the boy along with him to the office, but only after a lot of persuasion from Alpha.

Mr. Alpha Sasah closed the door after they had left and that was the last time he saw Mr. Bamba in the school. Mr. Bamba returned to his former school and took back his department headship.

Alpha had been in a middle school where the teachers were picking his brains, and using his teaching materials he had developed. But these were of the favored skin color and earned the respect of the school administration and the students, while Alpha was put through a torturous ordeal each day, with open hostility and irritating comments from students in class and avoiding attitudes from fellow teachers who thought that the classroom was not for people with an accent like Alpha.

Alpha had to endure it all because he was a substitute teacher, and had no voice, no one wanted to talk to him or heard anything from him and the administration could have him replaced at any time by just a simple phone call. And yet he needed the money to maintain his family.

Lethargy was evident in every school. A head of department in a middle school confessed in a training day group discussion that he hated reading and writing. That he never wrote anything on the board, and that he did not read students work. He would rather have students rewrite the same material three times and he will give a grade for the third and final draft, by simply looking at the handwriting and neatness of the essay.

Alpha got to connect this statement with what he overheard students saying "I got an "A" grade for doing nothing. I pretended to be rewriting the same stuff and submitted it for an "A" grade. But the black students did do their work all the time, but they talked a lot in class and so they got "D", "E " and " F " grades.

This was confirmed later by a student at a popular high School. Alpha was making a puzzle and two students came up to him to find out what he was doing. They thought he was writing up some one as the usual case teachers' only spent time writing up students for punishment. He explained to them that he was not only doing that but he was also writing a novel called "Blackman: too hard for you." he took a floppy disk and explained to the students that it was about how black people were downgraded, no matter how hard they tried. They always got failing grades.

"This was true you know" said the ninth grade boy. "In my history class, I have never done any work at all. No class work, no homework, nothing at all but I did not talk in class, and the teacher gave me a "B+ "grade.

You see that girl," pointing to a black girl busy doing her class work. "She sat next to me in my history class. She did all her class work every day, and all her home work, but she got an "F" grade all the time. I did not think it was fair to give me a high grade and that girl who worked ever so hard in class every day to get a failing grade. But that was how things went" he said and walked away. The bell rang for the end of the period.

This was by no means an isolated incident in the system as a whole, he thought. Alpha had learned as he went from one school to another the mountains of inefficiencies that existed and that were dragging the system to the point where we were at the very bottom in terms of standards and achievements. Hypocrisy, solidarity with the lords of the manor was the catholic truth for survival or faced obliteration from the institutions. But substitute teachers carry the can for these inefficiencies as they were used as smoke screens by authorities to hide the realities.

We believed that things could get better if each school had the option to select its students, it would make a world of difference on the quality, attitude, comportment of the students.

We felt too that the learning environment served to motivate or demotivate the students to work hard and produce quality end products of graduates not the product of inadequate present day out put. Even in cases of discipline, There were schools in the same environment and the same system within the same catchment area where students, discipline and motivation was ninety eight percent and no police in the school compound and not a private school by definition. But in the same vicinity and the same catchment area with students of similar circumstances schools needed police visible presence all the time. There were mountains of disciplinary problems, you could not tell the differences between children dressed to go to bed at night, going to a football field and going to school all in the name of freedom. Why do teacher and administrators in some schools spent most of their time on discipline and needed the police for help and yet teachers and administrators in others schools in the same environment have no major disciplinary problems and all the students were motivated to learn, respected themselves and every one else around them.

We were of the opinion that it was possible to modify the behavior, attitude and motivation towards education of public school students in Sarawali city.

We felt that to achieve this end there should be a new generation of students was needed.

The principals of good schools in terms of discipline, student motivation and comportment as examples of effective management in similar settings should be cloned.

The present status quo of who was who in the system and the hierarchical pattern, its stringent maintenance and the paying of homage to some people in the system to keep the lid on should be looked at from the tails end.

The reasons for this suggestion of changes was that the quality of students their motivation, out look and behavior would be influenced by the administrative step up, the environment and their friends and relatives above them. Those hardened old students who already knew how to manipulate the system to their own advantage and what you could get away with socialize in the corridors and out of school injecting into the fresh men a heavy dose of the behavior and attitudes and comportment you witnessed each day in school. This gave rise to a continuation of the same behavior and attitudes perhaps to an extended degree of what went on in our schools each day.

We felt that it was the case with little doubt that the school administration has a lot to do with the outlook of the institution, the quality of programs and the discipline inside the building.

The end result of the present state of affairs would be the same students with similar quality of output would be rolling out of the educational conveyor belt in the future and blaming it all on the teachers.

The absence of many fundamental issues that needed to be addressed and either ignored or over looked by the policy makers and the attitude of "I am the boss you accept it or you were out of here" had persisted and had corroded the very foundation of sound education.

The idea of Godly status for some individuals within the system had not only reduce good governance and the idea of "to please the boss syndrome" and the present day production of half baked product and swelling the pyramids of smart kinds who could not impress anyone with academic prowess except the legal educational anthem of "I have it clean and dry."

The idea of using the who know you anthem in the system backed by favoritism, nepotism and the prominence of color coding discretely should give way to quality management founded in excellent semi autonomous institutions under the same umbrella. We felt that the present cohort of academia had ran out of steam and ideas and were just plunging on like a marooned man on a desert island hoping that things would change for the better some day in the distant future.

CHAPTER TWO

THE SCHOOL SYSTEM IN Sarawali city was by no means isolated but a typical representation of the system of public education at large as observed generally by Alpha. Student comportment, motivation, dedication to school work, dress and behavior were generally typical of public schools. Private schools like catholic Schools and other private institutions did not only operate differently, but the quality of students, general attitudes, motivation towards learning were the opposite of what went on in our public schools as observed by Alpha.

Perhaps the general assumption that public education was free and so had very little value to those who received it while private education was not free and expensive and afforded by only the rich and people in good positions in society and therefore their children would value the education because it is paid for and quite expensive for some.

Substitution was a daily process as lots of teachers stayed away from impossible students who made the lives of both teachers' administrators and even their fellow students a hell hole each day. A lot of school teachers started off as substitute teachers before they were appointed into regular job positions by school administration. But this movement was by no means automatic by seniority but they were based on who knew you and your skin color.

People of color especially immigrants with foreign qualifications like Alpha have an assured place as substitute teachers only. It was obvious and certain that a black man, an immigrant with an obvious accent was sure to be on the dead end of any list of promotions in the system.

But stigmatization of all black people including students in these schools was a part and parcel of the system.

Alpha had been to a Middle School in the South of Sarawali city. There were these three black youths sitting in class doing nothing at all, while the rest of the class was working hard. He walked up to one of them, stood by him. The boy looked up at Alpha with cold eyes.

"Why were you not doing your class work?" Alpha asked the student calmly. The boy stormed with an angry voice.

"I am not doing no work, just leave me alone. Did not even talk to me go away" the boy was very angry and looked agitated.

Alpha said nothing, but waited until the boy cooled down and he asked him again in a soft brotherly voice what was wrong. The boy said in an angry voice, the teacher hated me. I did all my work every day, and she gave me an "F" grade all the time. I knew that I was going to fail even if I did all the work I would never pass this class. So I would not bother myself. We were black and so we were not expected to pass" he said with emphasis and an irritated voice.

The plague of disorder was evident everywhere. Alpha was in a school where teacher absences were up to 20% and sometimes more in some days and student absence could reach up to 35%. Student behavior was despicable at all times and these students ruled the school and the institution was more or less at these students' mercy.

Alpha was yet in another middle school, where the Principal confessed by a sleep of the tongue that may be it was a deliberate choice of students for his school by the school district placement office.

"Students who no other school wanted and who no one could control were sent to my school" he said in a disappointing voice. Students went round the school building banging doors and windows, slamming every open door, as they went from one floor to the other.

As Administrators chased these students round like a merry go round, they moved from one floor to another floor. They screamed on the corridors and forced doors to open and enter classrooms uninvited to cause confusion and then ran out. If the teacher tried to force them out, the teacher would get insults, damage to classroom property, especially substitutes who did not know their names and none of the students would give the names of these students. A veteran history teacher in this middle school said he left a large space in front of his classroom, because he constantly had students came in and disrupted his lessons.

No wonder you have administrators constantly patrolling the corridors to intercept those cutting classes, those who got permission to go to the bathroom and then wonder around the building but very little if any action was meted to these students encouraging them to continue behaving the same way.

School administrators were aware of the problems substitutes teachers faced in the classroom, but they often ignored these problems and pretended not to be aware of the problems. They used this as a smoke screen to punish the substitute teachers by blaming them as the ones responsible for the discipline problems in their schools in the first place.

Sometimes they used these problems as a yard stick to measure the substitute teacher's effectiveness and also as punishment for the disadvantaged substitute teacher like blacks with discrete negative recommendations to the district office.

They sometimes used the problems substitute teachers faced as a smoke screen to hide the inefficiency and failures of the school system and blamed the substitutes for inefficient class room management.

Substitution was and still an anathema in the wider school system.

Substitute teachers were discriminated on at every level of school administration, by teachers, students and even administrative support staff.

In the first instance, in those schools with assigned parking, with very few exceptions if any at all in Sarawali city, parking attendants refused to give parking spaces to Substitutes. Teacher who knew their colleague was absent would park in their lot to stop a substitute from parking in the spot. Alpha had had this problem many times and he had had three parking violation tickets because of that.

Regular teachers had prevented him as substitute from parking in absent teacher's parking lot. The incidents were not worth reporting any where because no one would listen or did anything about it or believed the substitute teacher especially if he was black with an accent.

Alpha had been told many times by park attendance and teachers that the parking lots were only for teachers and substitutes should park on the side of the street. Parking in unmarked spaces in the parking lot in some schools was a serious crime. The Substitute would get a red sticker put on his wind shield that was semi permanent parking violation warning and would take days to get rid of it as Alpha found out when he got one of those red stickers on his wind shield. An indication that you were not welcomed and you were not a teacher per se.

You the substitute dare not spoke out, because no one behind the desk would take you seriously especially if you were the usual black substitute with an accent. If you were bold enough to complain to an administrator or one of the secretaries, you would be told in an arrogant language that parking spaces were only for regular teachers. You had to accept what the Custodian said who would repeat the regular teacher preferences for parking spaces.

Alpha had overheard a secretary told another Substitute teacher that "Parking spaces were for teachers and administrator only." That was an indication yet again that a substitute was not a teacher, and therefore, he did not belong in the school.

The regular teachers and even administrators treated substitutes not only with contempt but with suspicion. The teachers would lock up all the teaching materials, leaving the Substitute nothing to handle, which was one of the sources of the substitute's discipline problems. Sometimes no lesson plans were left behind, not even a pen to write with or lined papers for the students to use. The work left behind in most cases if any at all would be for a third of the lesson time. Where an assignment was left behind by a conscientious teacher some students would complete the assignment in a few minutes. When the teacher left in a hurry students would not tell the Substitute what they had done the previous day. That was quite understandable because most students never knew what was going on in class and what the teacher was doing. They were only concerned with grades, the one and only important item in students' school agenda and even the school and the system.

Students would have nothing to do, and so they would resort to indiscipline.

In one middle school, the Principal made a directive that "No Substitute was to be permitted to use the computer when the teacher was away.' This notice was placed in every classroom door.

In another middle school, the white lady teacher opposite Alpha's classroom was spying on what Alpha was doing through a peep hole at the end of the school day. He knew what she was doing after a black female student had told Mr. Alpha that the white teacher was spying on him through a peep hole, but he decided to ignore her.

He was writing some pages of his novel "A taste of the American dream. "The students knew what he was doing because he told them and the curious students had read some of his writings. But this white lady teacher thought he was up to something not good and being black in a white teacher's classroom spurred the investigation to have something to talk about when her colleague came back the next day, and so she kept an eye on him all the time. She moved into the next classroom after all the students had left to have a good view of Alpha. Even though Mr. Alpha knew what she was doing he pretended not to notice her presence by the door.

When Mr. Alpha turned the lights off to go home she walked quickly across the corridor into her classroom banged the door closed.

Mr. Alpha laughed, shook his head and just left without saying a word.

As a Substitute teacher, you were not allowed to conduct Laboratory investigations. Most lessons either technical or scientific were all taught in ordinary classrooms all the time.

Alpha was not allowed to conduct laboratories in the school, even though he was a long term substitute, better trained than the privileged teachers and he was much more experienced. He was more qualified in his subject than most teachers in the department and he had international experience which none of the teachers had but being black with an accent put him in a special category of disadvantaged substitutes that stayed where he was for the foreseeable future.

Most teachers in every school had only the first degree and a masters degree was optional and for promotion prospects and for obtaining professional teacher status. The department head handed Alpha a memo, saying that he could only conduct laboratories if students did have laboratory gowns and goggles. These were items that had not been supplied to his room and other rooms over the years and may never be supplied.

But students' vague understanding of the subject as basically the dissection of some organism, be it a frog, fish, pig etc. Laboratory work was not part and parcel of teaching in some schools as Alpha had observed because teaching a practical subject in an ordinary classroom meant for English or social studies was not ideal.

But teaching a practical subject in an ordinary classroom did not seem quite right for the students and even the teacher but that was how the system had operated and Alpha was by no means in a position to change long standing tradition being a substitute teacher.

"When would we do dissection?" was all that students asked all the time. The fact that teachers did the same thing repeatedly, and students came to school and expected to do nothing gave rise to demotivation.

You often saw a large number of students coming to school, dropped by their parents or walking along the corridors with their hand in their pockets or carrying nothing. They went home with no work to do and some of them hardly read anything even in school and so the life style of hopelessness.

The whole school system accepted homework as the basic and core of the school education. Students went home to do only homework which in some cases lasted only for a few minutes and many students were reluctant to do anything else after they completed their homework. "I have done my homework, I have nothing else to do" was all that you heard from most students.

It was not uncommon to have students who graduated from even high school who have never read a complete chapter of any text book. The most common language accepted by every one in the system was homework. The idea accepted and used in the system by every one was that students only learn by doing homework, no matter how short it was.

Reputable companies advertised for helping students do their homework to improve on their school grades. But Alpha often wondered how doing just homework would improve significantly somebody's academic standing without any other work but research and theory here seemed to justify that end result. We are of the opinion that since teachers' grades were all that mattered in the system and nothing else, getting a good grade from the teacher as indicated above could be the result of where we were in world academic standing.

It seemed to us that all that a student needed to do well in school and graduated with good school records was doing just home work in the house. It never mattered whether the student spent only minutes doing the work, a relative or a friend did it for him did not matter. As long as the homework was presented the required grade would be given. Homework is a big deal even those who were pioneering a scheme to pay students by the hour to study were talking about helping students did their homework.

The fact of the matter was that hard working teachers became very unpopular with students, giving rise to disciplinary problems.

"Why did we have to do work every day? You were stupid. You gave too much work, I hated you, I hated this classroom, because you always came in here to do work were some of the students statements of discontent.

Give us a break man like Mr X. he gave me a good grade for doing no work". Few people within and without the system really believed that these were some of the comments you would hear from students all the time and no one would believe them because they were not part of a celebrated research report.

Those hard working teachers would then be seen by administrators as not doing their job, because they had disciplinary problems in their classrooms from revolting students.

The general yard stick used to measure a teachers effectiveness had always been and would continue to be the number of referrals written by the teacher and calling an administrator for help with disciplinary issues in his room. The best and most effective teachers by administrative definition were those teachers who did not call for help and rarely write referrals, even if they did not teacher at all.

Thus the teachers who kept students quiet all the time, but did nothing were seen as the good and best teachers by school administration. Simply keep the students quiet was all that mattered to administrators, because they would not have to come to drag a student out of your classroom and they would not have to read any referrals from you.

The absolute equation for any school administrator would be, no referrals and no disciplinary problems therefore equal to the best teachers in classroom management and general output. Teaching or not teaching was generally not important as there was no yard stick to measure your performance and pedagogical effectiveness.

Mr. Alpha was once told by a female Guidance Councilor one morning after pulling him out into the corridor outside his classroom (This was an "A" student. She got "As) in all her classes except yours. You should do something about it please" she then left.

Alpha looked at his mark book. The particular student had not handed in seven out of eight home works but she was generally quiet and did not act silly in class. She had handed in only three out of twelve class room assignments and non was worth a passing grade. "I would not give her an "A" for this poor work. She did not get a "C+" in any of the work she handed in so far.

But these were the things that led to one being booked in the black book of the administrators if you tried to exert your own authority.

By giving most students higher grades than necessary, administrators would put your name in their good books since there were no complaints from the students and no referrals from you and nothing to worry about your classroom was all that administrators required of good teachers by definition.

But giving very good grades to students who did not deserve the grades would put them at par with deserving students making the grading system meaningless.

But believe it or not that would put the teacher on the negative side of things if he decided to argue with an administrator or refused to do as told by the administrator.

At the same time if one was too strict with grades, and tried to justify his work either, one would be labeled as not doing his work well, or they built innuendos around him.

All grades were entered in pencil and subject to changes more often than not, giving rise to the poor performance evidenced in District and State tests.

This was an indication that school grades were not compatible with actual performance or output by these students. This status quo would remain the same as long as administrators in schools and elsewhere were more concerned in pleasing favorite students or their parents with false high grades that did not translate into reality.

Clever teachers knew that the principle of just keep quite and did as you were told syndrome applied in the classroom and for your very survival.

Otherwise the teacher would be seen as insubordinate and unwanted comments could be put in the teacher's personal file in the head office without his notice which would affect his teaching career forever.

And so teachers sometimes pleased the school administrators against their will helping to build the big pile of hypocrisy that was the dominant and determining factor for survival in the school system.

Alpha tied up this statement from the school administrator with the grade changes that went on most of the time. "F" and "E" grades he gave to some students had been changed to "As" and "Bs".

He remembered been warned by a veteran Special Education Teacher that he should keep a copy of the grades he gave to all his students, because its very common to change grades and called it a computer mistake.

Alpha had been approached by a former student during vacation on the street and in the mall saying "you told me you gave me a "B" grade, but I got an "F" grade in your class"

He remembered that this particular student was doing well in class, and to get an "F" grade was unusual. This was very common though, but very difficult to justify to the student on the street. But the arbitrary grades were a common phenomenon.

There was a common understanding that school administrators knew that teachers did not teach, but low noises and no disciplinary write ups and calls for help from your classroom were all indicators officials watched for all the time from individual teachers.

The password was "Keep your students in your class, make very few write ups" and teach nothing, you would still be in the list of very good teachers. Teaching was a secondary matter and not all that important as far as school administration was concerned.

This was confirmed by a statement from the Principal of one very large and ailing school. He said in a Professional training session, held regularly. "If your students did not succeed, you would still be paid. You would still keep your job, but try something different each day."

Students who disrupted classes, or walk out of class without permission, or walked up and down corridors were treated with leniency. They were given fifteen minutes detention which most of them did not attend anyway. Students sent to focus room for more than one day, simply stayed home to avoid Focus detention and that ended the punishment and nobody would ask a question.

A teacher in the lower rumps of the ladder who was like prop roots and substitute teachers would not dare ask questions about any issue because their presence was hardly recognized by administrators.

Students were given work that lasted only a few minutes. Some did not do it, others copy from friends, and yet others asked a friend to do the work for them. Administrators knew about these problems, but simply turned a blind eye to them.

If you tried to correct these problems, you became unpopular to students and administrators and a target yourself. You faced the possibility of been black listed by the school administrators.

In most cases, what was written in school rules and regulations rarely matched with what went on in the building. As a teacher, and especially a substitute teacher, you have to learn to be quiet, write as few disciplinary reports as possible if at all and be very generous with grades for your students.

But in reality who actually cared about the district or state tests since the students the parents and the teacher hardly took notice of those results, only the school administrators and the statistical annual exercise.

The teacher needed his job and giving inflated grades to please an administrator would not hurt the teacher and would actually not affect the school per se, it helped the child to graduate with a diploma. But that did not seem right by any shape or form but it was most welcomed by the student and the administration and you would be seen as a cooperative teacher who understood the students' needs.

Students protesting for grade changes were a very common phenomenon as Alpha observed. You the teacher was entitled to tell the students their grade when they asked for it, but there was no guarantee that what you told the student in class was what would appear on the report card sent home; since these grades were modified for various reasons like infringing on school rules and some other criteria.

Alpha came to know about this when a bright and hard working student in one of his classes had her grades down sized for fighting in the corridors and this was the very student who approached Alpha in the mall questioning her grades. This was a second punishment it seemed, after the suspension for fighting but who really took notice of the injustice and mistakes.

It was five years since Alpha was first appointed. He had become a seasoned substitute teacher going to a different school each day. His African colleagues from one school to another kept asking him "why were you still substituting?" 'I have no idea" would be the obvious reply since had no one to lobby for him, he knew no body in the head office and so he was entirely at the mercy of the big boys who saw him as an outsider and an alien.

"But you were a certified teacher in your subject area and there were schools without certified teachers. That was quite strange" they would say. But his circumstances, his position and standing in the social strata would not make him a viable candidate even for consideration for a regular job and so he would continue to be a substitute teacher.

One teacher in a Middle School would always say to Alpha each time they met "try and get on. You have to work hard at it and keep trying."

A teacher in a receptacle school for drop outs or would be dropouts once told Alpha after seeing him over the years. "Look I was very lucky to get this job. I was not up to it, nor had the qualification for the job, but I got employed anyway. I had been teaching chemistry for a long time here." Alpha knew that his Caucasian color gave him the job, because he belonged to the most favored employable group.

It was Monday morning Alpha was called out and told to take up a vacant position in the school not far from a special school in Sarawali city and not far from the cream of the action.

He went to school and found himself in the same classroom he was before. The head of department welcomed him back and told him that the teacher had resigned. This was confirmed by two other teachers and the Guidance Councilor for the team. The secretary told him to register late comers, when he should be attending a planning meeting. He knew that something was wrong.

The assistant principal saw him and ignored him. Alpha said Hi to the assistant Principal but he did not answer. An hour later the secretary came to Alpha and told him that he would be called out the next morning for another assignment.

He went out and told his next door colleague Mr. Dream, who earlier in the morning gave him a hearty welcome back with a big hug. "You better see the union representative in the school, because I did not understand this.

The two white colleagues who were showing a cold shoulder to Alpha conferred.

The special Education teacher came into the classroom, and on seeing Alpha showed open disappointment with body language and expressions. She left without saying a word to Alpha. The female white colleague who did not like Alpha made faces at him, she avoided eye contact with him.

Mr. Coupee the assistant Principal came by and Mr. Habaroni who was the cock of the team the alpha male in the section and also the oldest member in the school called Mr. Coupee and asked him if Alpha had come back to the position. Mr. Coupee said "no" by shaking his head left to right. Mr. Habaroni walked away with his hands high up with joy and happiness, laughing joyfully into Ms. Dodge's room to tell her the good news. Mr. Alpha could hear them rejoicing. They were joined by the special education teacher and Mr. Habaroni came out saying aloud "thank God. I knew it, no way. I felt light inside me now." He walked into his room.

Mr. Alpha tried to find the union representative, but he could not locate him all day.

Next morning, Alpha was called out again. He protested saying "you told me yesterday that that was a vacancy. The Substitute placement officer told Alpha that, it was indeed a vacancy, but the Principal said he did not want you in that position. I did not know why, you may want to talk to him and find out why" she said at the other end of the phone

Mr. Alpha went to another school, and at the end of the school day he went to the union office to complain. A complaint form was filled in, and then the man dampened Alpha's hopes by saying that it was not unusual for school Principals to request preferences for their school, that his case was not uncommon. Alpha left with less hope than when he came in.

As he walked out of the door to the car park, he knew that that was the end of the matter.

The union officer himself was more racist than Alpha thought from his body language and the way he talked to Alpha in a dismissive attitude. As Alpha expected, the complaint never bore any fruits. Nothing was done about it, and nothing was ever communicated back to him as feedback.

It was more than a waste of his time to go to the union office in the first place, because he was not on the favored list of people that should be complaining and be attended to and got their complaints looked into.

Alpha applied to one of the mushroom schools sprouting out. He went to see Ms Ovambo for a reference. She was the assistant Principal when he was teaching at Huntingdon High school. She was pleased to see Alpha after a while from her body language. She looked at him with surprised looks a bright face and a welcomed posture "were you still substituting?" she asked Alpha.

"Yes" he replied.

"Woo why have they not appointed you to a regular position up to this time?" she asked with an anxious voice. She took the phone called two men downtown. She left a message for each. "I tell you what I would talk to some one in the District office "come see me tomorrow afternoon."

Alpha left, but he knew that there were people of Spanish origin who have been substituting for more than seven years without appointment. His case was not a one off case in general. It was the case in this district in particular to push people forward who had some one to lobby for them.

Alpha was told by the assistant principal with favored color and credentials that he substituted for only one year and three years later he was promoted to where he was, an exposition of the overt principle of who was who and who knew who as the driving force in getting a job and promotions.

This man had told Alpha that substitution was a difficult job and that the one year he did it was more than enough. He said he would never want to do that again and that he was very lucky to be appointed a regular teacher and then he was appointed assistant principal in a middle school in the south of the city.

Next day Alpha went back to see Ms Ovambo he waited outside the office for a while, she came out in a hurry quite busy it seemed and she saw Alpha standing in the corridor. "I have talked to Betty Jullant, to look into your file and see what had been put in it that had held up your appointment. She was going to get back to me with the details.

One week past, Alpha went back to see Ms Ovambo in this extra large high school. He waited outside and she came out with a student behind her.

"Hi Alpha I was busy, but guess what; someone had a write up in your file. I would have you write a complaint letter to Jullant. She also suggested that Alpha went to the district and examined his file himself as a right.

That was the forbidden crime Alpha committed and paid for it very dearly. By protesting through another black person had made himself a black sheep in the white flock of an overt racist institution.

The usual protocol was that you did not complain about anything because complaining was equal to challenging the status quo and pushing yourself into more disadvantages. But Alpha did not know the order of things and no one advised him about the repercussions of challenging the status quo.

Alpha decided to go and look at his file.

After three cancellations of appointments, he eventually got to look at it. Mrs. Shanana told Alpha that he had some orange cards in it. He read through the two cards in her written more than three years back. "Call tomorrow so that I would give you the phone number of Romeo Anderson who was the subject coordinator."

Why would she not give me the phone number now when she knew that it was very difficult to reach some one in there offices by phone? Alpha tried to get this phone number before he left but she told him that she was too busy. He left and after the usual hypocrite laugh and niceties.

But why would I not get these phone numbers right now while I was still here and considering the difficulties one had to go through to get to talk to anyone in these apparently busy offices he told himself.

Alpha went home and had to give up after six calls without any answer and he left one message after another without receiving any call back.

One month past, he wrote the complaint draft letter, and dropped it at Ms Ovambo's office. He went to see her two days later, and he waited for half an hour to see her. She came out with a student by her side walking along the corridor, and talking to the student.

Alpha followed them behind, she turned round and told Alpha that she was busy, but she would redraft the letter which he should send to Betty Jullant. "I was in contact with Betty" she said and walked on. Alpha slowed down and decided to walk to the door near the car park.

In the afternoon after Alpha came back from school, Betty called to make an appointment for Alpha to come over and meet with her in her office. Alpha went to the office to meet with Betty. He waited for a while and then he was called in. As he sat down the most senior officer in the department came in. His attitude and behavior were negative and very evasive as he tried to defend the write ups in Alpha's file and told Alpha to get a letter from one of the Principals supporting him for a job appointment.

The man knew fully well that Alpha would not get that letter because he had not worked long enough in any one school for a Principal to write that letter for him.

The letter would commit the Principal to employ Alpha the black man with an accent as a regular teacher. The man left abruptly after making the statement.

Ms Jullant went out to fetch Alpha's personal file. They went through the file together. "There were two orange cards in your file" she told him. "One of the orange cards came from the Humphrey Academy in the West of the city."

Alpha looked through the card which the officer in charged had refused to let him handle. He explained that he was there for only one day. That there were no lesson plans as usual, no seating plans, and no class lists left for him and no teaching schedule. The white Principal Dr Humberg wrote the time schedule on a scrap of paper and gave it to him and said nothing to him what so ever.

The rule as it was in theory was that a substitute must be in a school for at least one full week before they could write a report on him. "It was both unfair and unreasonable for her to write that report, because she knew what was going on in her school. But the fact was that whatever the principal wrote about a teacher especially a black man and a substitute teacher for that matter would be accepted as the whole truth by the district without contest by the teacher and without the knowledge of the teacher concerned. That was one good example of school administrators blaming the substitute teachers for their own ineffective management policies, impeaching their own frustrations and smoke screening a totally defunct arm of a sinking flag ship.

It was a hard fact that school administrators were hiding behind their dysfunctional administration and bullied the substitute teachers like Alpha. He was the black sheep and the cause of the problems in their schools and so punishing the substitute teacher with negative reports pretending to show that they the administrators were doing their jobs right. But these untrained and unqualified staff supplied to them as baby sitters were the problem themselves one administrator declared.

The write ups on the substitute teacher were nothing more than a camouflage to hide the inefficiencies in the school system, the inadequacies in these institutions and the failures of some of these principals to meet the basic standards for adequate education for the students. They were impeaching their short comings to the substitute teachers like Alpha as the cause of the deficiencies and the problems that existed in these schools.

The teachers and people along the administrative line knew about the existence of these deficiencies but were afraid to speak out for fear of their jobs and positions. By blaming the substitute teachers as the cause of the problems, they hid away their ineffectiveness.

Substitute teachers were being punished for obvious inefficiencies in these schools and the system that propped the lords of the manor but we felt that these were nothing more than smoke screens to cover the actual bad management of these institutions which every one concerned turned a blind eye to.

The substitute teachers were thought to be inefficient especially black substitutes like Alpha even though the regular teachers were denying the substitute teachers the tools they needed to do their job effectively compounding the problem and helping indirectly to prove the inefficiency if the substitute teachers.

The school administrators knew that the regular teachers were not doing their contracted jobs effectively and they were not providing the tools the substitutes needed to teach. But because they were white and the favorites in most cases and some of these teachers could bring down an administrator and destroy his future because of their inner connections, no one therefore cared and just ignored the fundamental problem and let sleeping dogs to lie.

And there was no mechanism in place in the system to assess the effectiveness of individual teachers in any of the institution. The administrators could do very little about the effectiveness of individual teachers considering union politics, favoritism and behind the scene support of certain individual teachers, the politics of who was who in school.

This was also compounded by the existence of cliques in most institutions and being in a clique with those that mattered in the institution put the teacher in an advantaged position. The fact that the politics of who was who made some school administrators scared of antagonizing some teachers and correcting any of their short comings. The politics in the school influenced even the way the administrators dealt with some students for fear of their own very positions and the negative out come of some action by these administrators.

As a result, some of the actions of certain teachers were over looked by administrators and the substitute teacher was in the receiving end and got the blame squarely in the end because he had no protection and no one in his favor.

And so any one could take a short at Alpha the substitute teacher, since a teacher reporting a substitute to the administration would spell disaster for the substitute. He therefore carried the can for the institution where every Tom and Harry would empty their frustration whole sale without looking back on the substitute as an individual person.

Mrs. Jullant looked at Alpha with eyes of concern these write ups for teachers would be kept in his file for ever especially a black man like Alpha with an accent, an added disadvantage.

The other card came from the Meridian middle school on Calvino Street. Alpha said he spent two weeks in the Focus room.

"Oh, you were having students whom other teachers did not want in their classrooms?" said Betty. Did any one tell you that you should not be a focus teacher because you were not a regular teacher in the school and you would not know who you were dealing with? No Alpha replied.

"Did any one ever told you to come to the office to discuss these orange cards and made suggestions on what you needed to do about the write ups?" she asked with a curious voice.

"No" Alpha replied. "I never even knew that there were orange cards in my official file in the district office.

"The rule was" she went on, " as soon as they received these cards, they should call you to discuss the contents with you and made suggestions on how to remedy the points highlighted on the card." she said quietly. She looked at Alpha with stern eyes and tightened lips an indication that something was definitely going wrong somewhere.

"Nobody ever called me and nobody ever told me about these cards in my file." Alpha said quietly, but with a nervy voice.

"That was quite strange" she said in a croaky voice.

"Secondly, these cards had been sitting in your file for more than three years now when they should have been discarded at the end of the school year. This was the middle of the fourth year and they were still in your file." she said in an upset voice.

It was a strange meeting, and Alpha was not aware of what was going on behind the closed doors.

The white lady whom Alpha came to see in order to view his file came quietly to see who Alpha had the meeting with. Alpha's file was on the desk opened and Mrs. Jullant was holding the orange card in her hand which was like shooting yourself in the foot.

The meeting between Alpha and another black person in the administrative office had its own negative out comes on Alpha's position and increased his disadvantage and further pushed his chances of changing his present position further down the list of impossibilities.

Alpha remembered that in the teacher's contract there were sections that highlighted these cards and the length of time they should remain in the teacher's file.

It was a contractual agreement that no negative items on a teacher's character or work should be put in his file. But these cards had been in his file for nearly five years. "These were the cards the Director mentioned earlier on in the meeting when he said Alpha had cards in his file.

She looked at Alpha again with searching eyes. "I tell you what; we would see what happened after the Job fair on April 30. There would be lots of openings then. Alpha knew that the rules in the teacher's contract applied only to those teachers in the good books of the rank and file of the administration and not a black person like himself who was also a substitute teacher in addition.

Alpha again made a serious mistake that was very costly in terms of his job. He applied for a job in one of the mushroom school sprouting in the city he needed yet again a reference but since he had not been in one school for more than one week it was not easy to get any principal to give him a reference. His problems had no end and no light at the end of the tunnel.

Alpha went to attend an interview in a chartered school by route 681. The principal told Alpha that they were paying him too much. She was not happy with the pay scale for Alpha which she indicated. Alpha told her that he had two Masters Degrees, three teacher training certificates and nearly two decades teaching experience. She acknowledged that but she was not impressed by the certificates and she did not believe that as a black person like Alpha should be paid for all those qualifications. And after the interview Alpha never heard from her again.

The journey would now take us through individual schools Alpha substituted in the Sarawali city over the years.

These were first hand experiences, as Alpha went through the very hard task of a substitute teacher in an environment where Alpha had all the disadvantages that made the life of even the most determined, resilient and most motivated workaholic would be reduced into nothingness, gasping for understanding, simple reasoning and human dignity.

Please read on and enjoy the value of determination to succeed in the face of overwhelming odds in a messy and sometimes chaotic environment where Alpha and people like him were forced to stay behind an iron wall of racism and apartheid shrouded in the popular slogan "an equal opportunity employer."

CHAPTER THREE

IT WAS EARLY MONDAY morning Alpha went to school full of energy and determination to succeed and to make an impression for himself. This was my first taste of teaching in an American school Alpha said to himself. He got to the school, parked his car on the side of the street and he went into the office to sign up and he received his home room folder and rushed upstairs looking for his room.

After a bit of looking around and asking for his room number he was pointed to the door and he eventually got into the room. He found nothing on the teacher's desk, he walked up to the teacher next door joyfully but the man looked at Alpha with eyes for any alien invading a city.

Hi Alpha greeted him with a broad smile and tried to find out about the teacher who was next door and the work he had left behind but he received a cold response and no adequate answer as the teacher pretended to be busy to avoid talking to him.

That was not a good sign to begin with but since he had not talked to anyone in the building yet he shook his shoulders and turned round and walked out without another word.

He walked back into his room and hoping to get ideas of the study program from the students. But as usual he knew that students generally would not tell you the truth about what they had done. Most of the students were lazy and would not be following the progress of the lessons and the program as a whole.

In fact most students in normal classrooms would not know what the teacher was doing each day and so most of them would not tell you where they were and where they were going with the study program.

This was because they would not have read the chapter in the text book and even if they had but the majority of them did not understand what they had read. And some of them would have pretended to be reading so they would actually not know the progress of the study program.

It was quite common that students would only open to the page where the exercises were and they would go ahead and do those exercises by guessing, or copying the answers from their friends.

And sometimes they would ask the teacher cunningly to explain to them what the question were all about so that the teacher would end up giving them the answers to the exercises there by spoon feeding them.

Alpha continued to search his surroundings for clues of what he had to do.

He found nothing and there were no indicators in the room to give him clues as to the study program and the text books were in a total mess and he was trying to decipher what to do and where to begin when he heard the bell.

The morning bell rang three times and it was home room time, the students came into the classroom noisily and in disorder.

"Were you the new Substitute teacher?" asked a boy who looked and dressed like a gangster. Alpha could not believe his eyes, the way the boy dressed. Was this how students in this country dressed for school he asked himself? One boy had an open chest; his nearly faded blue jeans were half way down his legs, below the waste line. His underwear was all up his flat stomach. He dragged his legs to keep the trousers (pants) in place. He had two pairs of under wear of different colors, one slightly above the other so that every one could see that he had two under wears.

A voice told him that this was not Europe where students dressed neatly with school uniform and a white shirt, neatly ironed trousers (pants) with a tie and black shoes; this was America where everything was the opposite of what he knew and got used to in Europe.

"What was your name anyway?" the boy went on. "Alpha" he replied with a smile, looking at the boy with amazement.

In came another boy, dressed in a similar fashion. "Fuckin hell what was this man doing here?" he said as he walked to his seat.

The first boy ran out and shouted "we have another substitute. A black Ass this time"

Both his hands were up in the air like a football fan celebrating a win.

All the students came in, some sat in their seats, others on the desks, making ear deafening noises.

Alpha stood quietly, looked round. One boy came up to him quietly and talked to Alpha in a low voice.

"Sir, you think you would be able to control these students? This was the worst class in the school. They would try to drive you crazy. You have to watch out; there were very bad boys in this group. Some had stayed for the third time in the same class. They were not coming to school to learn anything, but to cause trouble and they would drive you mad." He walked back to his seat. He sat quietly, his hands over his mouth looking straight forward.

One big boy walked up to him like a drunkard, with a green hand towel hanging from his back pocket, put his hands on the boy's desk, and then looked at the boy in his eyes." Hay white boy, what were you saying to the teacher, the Dude? He asked in a deep voice. He was the oldest boy about seventeen years old and biggest in the class of eleven year olds. The little boy was scared because he was eleven and very tiny compared to the big boy twice his size in height and weight.

The bell rang for the morning exercises. Every one was talking on top of their voices. Alpha got up, looked round with the hope that the students would quiet down but none of it. He beat the table with the duster the level of noise went down suddenly, and then went up again.

You have to have respect for the flag, you have to have respect for the school rules, and you needed to respect yourself.

It was time for the pledge to the flag and you were all talking on top of your voices. What type of behavior was that? What impression were you giving me of yourselves? If you did not have respect for the flag what type of people you think you were.

One boy got up. "Excuse me, you did not scream at us for any reason. You have no authority to scream at us. What you thought you were, we were not your children, my mom did not scream at me. There was no reason why you should scream as us." He sat down and went on talking to his friend.

"Sit down" Alpha said in a raised voice. "You gave me a bad impression of yourselves. I expected you all to respect the flag and the school rules. I got a bad first impression of you all."

"Ah ah, not everyone in here was a bad student" shouted one girl from the back. "More than half the students in here were good students. We all knew those who made trouble and we all got blamed for it. That was not fair to blame the whole class for the sake of just a few boys who made trouble all the time and got away with it."

"Shut up Hailey" shouted a boy who stood by the window, looking down the street. "You were talking trash. We all made noise and disrupted the lesson anyway so you should not exclude yourself from it.

Mr. Alpha watched him, his name was Wahandro and all the teachers knew him. He disrupted each class every day. He had detention for every teacher each day, but he did not go to any detention, and he got away with it all the time.

He put us into trouble all the time" added Linda.

"Flipping heck, why did you give my name to the teacher? I would beat you up after school today, you wait.

I would for sure, you wait and see. I would wait for you outside the building." He stuck his finger at her.

Alpha called the home room attendance register after the noise went down but not completely as some students still talked in low voices.

"Were you going to be our teacher for ever?" asked one girl who sat in the front row next to Alpha's desk.

"Yes" he replied in a sharp tone with a smile.

"We have been having Substitutes all the time and I was sick of it because we were not learning anything. We got bored and then we got into trouble.

The boy in the second row behind the girl, a big and tall student and in his fifteenth year said in a protesting voice, "they picked on me all the time," everyone was picking on me. No one liked me in this school. I did not know why. Did you like me?" He asked looking at Alpha with eyes of caution.

Mr. Alpha looked at him with sympathetic eyes without saying a word.

"Mr. Alpha, he was telling a lie the teachers wrote him up for detention all the time which he never attended and he was either under suspension or in the Focus room all the time. He should be in Focus room right now, but he did not go there" the girl next to him said.

"I was not going to no Focus room. The teachers kept writing me up for no reason, they all hated me.

"Well Kwesito, I did not feel that the teachers hated you" said Alpha in a low voice.

"Yes, they did, honest" he said in an angry voice.

"The teachers were here to help you and all the other students at the same time. The teacher had a program; he followed and hoped to complete each lesson. If you did not obey the school rules and you prevented the teacher from completing what he set out to do. You were not following the school rules and you would be sent to the focus room, you got that clear?"

The teacher would not allow you to stop the lesson from proceeding. He would not let you prevent other students from learning." Alpha told him in a calm and soft voice.

"I hated this school" he stormed. "They kept giving me "E" and "F" grades. Some students did nothing at all, but they got good grades. I did not like anybody in this school. I hated this school" he stamped his foot, and stormed out of the room, banged the door with a loud sound.

The day ended without Alpha completing any one of the lessons he prepared.

Next morning Alpha came to school determined to exert control in class and teach the prepared lessons. The first period did not go so well. He caught two students trying to throw the text books over the window while he tried to write notes on the board.

The second period was no better; the students were wild and very noisy. He

had a fight in the middle of the lesson. He went to stop the fight in the midst of the commotion; Kwesito took a folder from the book rack by the side wall, and pushed it out of the partially closed window. Alpha saw him closing the window in a hurry and he went over to him and looked over the window and saw a shower of papers flying all over the place. Alpha scolded him, but he denied that he did it, and none of the students next to him said a word. No one admitted seeing him threw the file.

As a common denominator for everywhere in this country, it did not matter what it was, no one would say a word if he saw someone doing anything wrong. Alpha was shocked when all the students denied seeing him throw the file.

But Alpha came to understand that that was part of the American culture, not to say anything about what you saw to save your life, that of your family and relatives.

This was because speaking out on any issue would result in your sudden death or the death of any member of your family and so keeping your mouth shut and saying nothing would save lives including your own and you would not have committed any crime "Miranda rights."

By the time he came back to his desk after scolding the boy and the commotion that followed, the duster and chalk had gone from the blackboard. The dittos he put on his desk had gone as well. All the students were watching what Alpha was going to do. He called for help.

The principal came in, and all the students sat straight and quiet.

Mr. Kaliffa the Principal looked round. "Your behavior was disappointing. There were students in this group I did not know their names. Some of you I have seen nearly everyday. I have suspended some of you many times over. You went round each classroom, disrupting other students from their education. This was the third years in the same class for some of you, and there were no prospects that you were going to make it to high school this year around. Who threw the papers over the window?" He asked in a calm voice.

"Kwesito" said Mr. Alpha.

"Kwesito, you again" the Principal looked at him with cautionary eyes. This was the third incident this morning you just came back from three days suspension. You were to stay in Focus until your mom came to see the teachers." Mr Kaliffa told him.

"I was not going to focus room" he said forcefully and defiantly.

Mr. Alpha, write down the names of those disrupting your lesson. I would keep them after school today. If I had to come back here again, you all would have one hour detention after school today" he said in a sharp tone and left with his right hand directing Kwesito to follow him.

"Go Kwesito" shouted one girl next to him. "You were getting into more trouble, if you did not go with the Principal" she told him.

"I did not care" he replied stamping his foot.

Alpha went up to him. "It's the principal talking to you, you better go. He was waiting for you outside the room. You could do your work tomorrow.

He got up and walked reluctantly to the door.

"Did you have work for him?" Mr Kaliffa asked.

"Yes, I did" Alpha replied. He went to Kwesito's desk; his ditto was already folded into a paper ball and was under his desk. He took the ditto on the next desk to give to Kwesito.

"Its mine" complained Doris.

"I would give you another one" Alpha assured her.

Mr. Kaliffa left with the boy.

There was a period of silence. He went to the garbage box to look for the dittos; he bent over and took out the pile.

Next day was Wednesday morning. Alpha got to school a bit late. He ran upstairs after signing and, he opened the door in a hurry, he put his bag and register on the table and went out he stood by the door to receive the homeroom students.

The Principal came by and looked into Alpha's room. His bunch of keys was on the table. He went into the room took the keys and handed them to Alpha, saying "Never leave your keys on your desk. They would disappear and you would never find them again. I suggest you move your desk on this side of the room. You always needed to keep an eye on your desk while you stood outside to watch your students. You would not know what was going on; on your desk if you left it where it was. Feel free to do that. You would keep an eye on your valuable things that way. You needed your car keys to go home and enter into your house. This was a very valuable advice, consider it and he walked away.

Alpha rearranged the room at the end of the day.

It was the fifth period that was most challenging for Alpha. The class had a lot more older students and eleven of them were repeaters who were all fifteen years or older with tiny eleven year olds. It was also the period after lunch when some students had the chance to sneak out of the building and smoked and came to class with erratic behavior.

These big guys knew that they were going to flung it at the end of the year, some of them would be eighteen years old and would be leaving school anyway before September so they had nothing to lose with their behavior.

These guys were always on the wrong side of things in the school and where ever they were. All the teachers knew them but all the teachers could do was to write them up and gave it to the Principal but there was no effective method of correcting these students.

Mr. Alpha stood outside the door waiting for the class to come in.

The lot came in noisily and disorderly, running, screaming, pushing and subbing. One boy was carrying a girl on his back.

"How were you getting on with these students?" asked the teacher next door as she stood close to Alpha watching these students walked into Alpha's room.

"It was a difficult assignment" Alpha replied.

"It's not just you. I had been in this school for eleven years. Things were getting worst each year. Some of these students came to school drugged up. They had no respect for anybody. They knew that we the teachers had less power over them. They knew their rights and they knew what they could get away with, they got away with just anything and everything. Worst of it some of these students had repeated the same grade twice and were going to flung it again. Some of them were sixteen plus, among eleven year olds. It's not right" she said in a disappointing voice. "They exert negative influence in class.

And I tell you what it's the same set of students that were causing problems from one classroom to another. I had stopped writing them up, because it was a waste of time writing up the same students each day, every day and nothing seemed to change. If only they could get rid of just twenty students out of six hundred and more in the school, that would make our lives much easier. There you were the boss man" she told Alpha and walked away quickly into her classroom.

"But why could she not talk to me" he asked himself. He remembered that the Principal was the Lord of the Manor. He could make the life of any teacher miserable, by the teacher simply being on the wrong side of things.

"How were you today?" Dr. Elrado the assistant Principal asked.

"I was still trying to exert control so that I would be able to teach effectively. Period five was the most challenging group."

"I knew you have some students in that group that gave trouble to other teachers as well. Mr. Alpha, you would not believe it" dragging the word believe. "We have tried every method to get these boys to concentrate on their school work. The parents were here most of the time. Some parents had given up, and had stopped coming to see the teachers. We were fighting a lost battle, believe it or not."

"Hay what was up?" Benjie said as he came close to Alpha and the principal. He danced round and tried to hug the principal. "What?" he opened his hands wide "it's time to start your class lesson? The principal walked away.

Alpha got into his room, closed the door. He noticed that his mark book was gone. He opened the draws, looked round. The students watched, but said nothing. "Who took the mark book?" he asked. "I knew that those who did not do class work and played up all the time did take the mark book. They hoped to change their grades that way.

You might be surprised to know that I had a copy of the grades at home. If you changed the grades in the mark book, you would be wasting your time. The grades I had at home were the true grades I would be using,

Secondly, if I discovered that you had changed your grades, I would down grade you further for cheating.

Alpha was relieved when the bell rang and all the students rushed out.

The students knew that Alpha had no right to search their book bags, without an administrator present and so they all left without any action.

Alpha reported the loss of his mark book to the assistant Principal, and was asked to give names of students he suspected. The list would not yield anything Alpha thought and he decided to give some names anyway.

He looked round the room and everywhere without success. He knew that students who were going to flung the year were those who took the mark book with the hope that they could change the grades or had an excuse to get better grades by accusing the teacher that they had done well, but the teacher had failed them deliberately and requesting that they would want to see all their grades over the course of the term which Alpha would not have been able to produce on demand and so he would have had to readjust the grades and gave them better grades. But these grades would have no effect on the students standing at the end of the school year anyway.

It was Friday afternoon, after all the students had gone out of the building, when one of the good students Harry who had always helped him in class, asked questions, and told Alpha lots of things about the school and the behavior of other students and those Alpha should pay attention to for behavior problems brought the book, held it in his hand. He looked at Alpha, but he said nothing.

"My father was a Professor at the City College and my mom was a medical doctor at the main hospital" he told Alpha." Mr. Alpha here was your mark book. I saw it in the lockers. I begged the boy to give it to me. But I could not tell you who gave it to me. I have promised not to tell his name, before he gave it to me, I am therefore not telling you who took the book from your desk, so please did not ask. I brought it for you because I knew you were a good teacher, and came here to help us. But there were more bad students in our class than good ones. You should concentrate on us who wanted to learn. I was going to the Grammar school next year. I had to work very hard to get there. I have already been admitted for September."

"Thank you Harry. I appreciated your effort" he said to the boy softly.

"You welcome" he said and left. He walked out quietly and disappeared.

Alpha opened the book, looked at the grades, which had been changed. The "F" had been changed to "B" and "D" to "A". Alpha closed the book, put it in his briefcase and walked to the door. He closed the door and went home.

The next day was Monday and it was already afternoon, the middle of the forth quarter. Most of the students already knew which high school they were going to next September. He was looking at the mark book "you alright?" Mr. Dandy the assistant principal asked Alpha as he pushed his head through the door, holding both door fames with both hands. Alpha got up, walked to him and stood by him outside the door.

"I was troubled by the fact that most of my students hardly did any work at allow. They came in and just sat down and talked or did their own thing. Some did not even look at the class work. I could not understand this type of attitude. Besides I found it quite frustrating after preparing your lessons and the students did not take them seriously. Some of them simply folded the ditto into paper ball and threw across the room or made paper airplanes and flew them out of the window.

Some of these students sneaked out of the building and went outside during lunch break to smoke weed or took drugs and came back after lunch looking like sleep walking men.

"I understood what you were saying" he replied "did not worry about it. It was the usual pattern. The students worked hard in the first to third quarters, and relaxed in the fourth. Some of them had no interest in the school, and so they were not coming to school to learn. Most of them already knew that they have past and would be graduating Any grades you gave them now would not affect their overall cumulative grade point average very much. Besides that, they already knew that they have been placed in the high schools of their choice. They would be going to high school next school year. But we have to keep them, until they graduated in June or until they were eighteen years old. Which even came first I was sure you must find the system rather strange.

Our educational system was quite different from that in Europe. It would take you some time to get used to this system. You simply kept your cool, you would get used to it. You complained of some desks of some desks and chairs in bad condition."

They went into the classroom and Alpha pointed to some chairs whose plastic covering and foam had gone and all that were left was the lining held by the nails.

"These chairs were in pretty bad condition. We needed to change them right away "Mr. Dandy told Alpha. "This was America, the land of plenty. Help me take all of these chairs outside into the corridor. We would have a new set in here this afternoon.

Wednesday morning, Alpha was in the room with the usual classes and the same students with the same behavior.

The last bell for the end of the day rang and all was getting quiet, Alpha was preparing to go home. The door opened and in came two girls, Mabel and Jendy in the fifth period who had become fund of Alpha came in to talk to him and befriended him.

"Mr. Alpha, we came to talk with you, we promised we would help you keep the class quiet. Those boys disrupted your class everyday, but trust us, we would tell them to shut up. We liked you and we wanted you to be happy. But Mr Alpha why did you decide to come to this school? This was a bad school. It was a waste of your time and talent to teach in this school. You were better off in another school. There were too many bad kids in here, using drugs, smoking weed. They come to school drugged up each day. Some of them went outside during lunch break to smoke weed, or took drugs. That was why you had lots of problems with the afternoon classes."

"Well, I did not make that decision you know. The school department sent me here for the rest of the school year." He told the girls who seemed enthusiastic talking to Mr. Alpha.

We liked the opportunity to talk to the teacher personally and you Mr. Alpha was very receptive and quite ready to listen to us. They talked about many things including their grades, the High schools they were going to attend next school year, their interests and what they hoped to do after high school. The thought that Mr. Alpha as a very friendly man because teachers did not like to talk to students or had students come that close to them. Mr. Alpha we would do anything you wanted us to do for you to make your life in here happy, trust us we would challenge these bad boys in class and make them respect you." Alpha had to look at his watch, since the girls wanted to stay with him a lot longer even though he wanted to go home.

Alpha was in a faculty meeting the other day and they talked about an exhibition, They decided that the teachers brought in any items they wanted to exhibit for parents to see what their children had been doing.

Alpha thought it was time to impress the other teachers and parents, because teachers did not meet to talk or discuss what they were doing. Every teacher was doing their own thing inside their room. In the meeting which was held very rarely, since the school had to pay hourly rate for these meetings it was decided that the exhibits would be laid out in the west side of the corridor on the first floor opposite the Principal's office. The date and time were set for the exhibition. Alpha was a novice and knew nothing about School politics who was who and the daily joining and comings of the staff.

The teachers came with their exhibits to lay out, he brought all his work and laid it out and went back into his room. He came down half an hour latter and found that the teachers had moved all their stuff to another location without him knowing. All he could see was his own work. "What happened?" he asked himself. He did not know his way round the building very much since he was still new in the building and his class schedule did not give him time to explore any thing, nor visit any where. It was more of a strict military type schedule each day that left him with hardly any time other than the wish to go home when the last bell for the day rang.

The teaching schedule was very tight and there was no time on his daily teaching schedule for him to speak to any one or did anything during the school day, so he did not know where the exhibition had been moved to since the teachers did not talk to him for any reason. He decided to leave his work where it was as no one wanted to talk to him as the only black teacher in the building.

He found out that teachers had a negative attitude towards him as the only African teacher with an accent in the building and they all avoided him and did not even invite him to their department meetings.

It was graduation day for the eighth graders. Mr Bidden who was Alpha's next door teacher was in charge of the graduation. Alpha was very curious about the event and he came in the morning with his camcorder to record the ceremony.

It was his first middle school graduation ceremony. The graduation was in the Northern Polytechnic football Stadium. Parents and guests were arriving and they were directed into the Stadium.

Alpha did not know the route of the procession; he decided to ask Mr Bidden. "Excuse me Mr Bidden, which way were the students matching into the Stadium?" Mr. Bidden ignored Alpha's inquiry and said nothing to him by pretending to be busy. Alpha felt bad but he knew that he was a black man, that was what he should expect. Nobody talk to him except they had to, otherwise why border with a black man with an accent and the accent had a stinking sound in their ears. He was a substitute teacher anyway and generally a substitute teacher had no respect and all the teachers in the school did not think much of a substitute teacher and students too did not think much of a substitute teacher.

The students were already in the lines to go into the Stadium. One of the students wanted to talk to Alpha. "No talking in the procession lines" shouted Mr Bidden angrily. Alpha gave up, and decided not to ask the second time, lest he be embarrassed in the public.

It was time for everyone to move into the Stadium. He went through the side door directly opposite the school main entrance. He held his Camcorder, videoed the procession as students began to move towards the stadium. He thought they were going to pass by him. They went the other way. The teachers were tight lipped about everything and Alpha was seen as an outsider, a substitute and a black African man with a strong accent for that matter. Alpha was by no means considered a member of the school and so he should not be part of the graduation ceremony. Alpha had his Camcorder on the parents as they came into the Stadium through that side door.

The ceremony went on with one speech after another. Alpha had never witnessed this type of ceremony before. He was amazed at the elaborate graduation ceremony at the end of the Middle School the usual grand ceremony in the United States equivalent to University graduation elsewhere.

European and African students in their home countries only graduate from University with a University degree. Alpha realized that this was America where graduation ceremonies were held for children from head start to Kindergarten and all the way to University. The end of every course no matter how short or abridged there was always a grand graduation ceremony.

"Why did kids in the Kindergarten graduate just like University students, with speeches, matching with gowns and miters? No wonder every certificate in America was called a degree."

It was time for the students to receive certificates, scholarship awards, good behavior and hard work certificates to names just a few.

It was amazing that the word degree had no meaning here in America, as every body used it to mean just any piece of paper from any institution.

CHAPTER FOUR

IT WAS THE BEGINNING of a new school year and Alpha had been moved to this popular high school at the beginning of the school year as long term substitute. He got to school early and he felt welcomed by the secretary he went up to his room in the fifth floor. Alpha found a lot of textbooks in the room all over the place. The Latino man who was also teaching the same subject in the same room was not happy to give up one of his class to Alpha. Alpha could not believe the body language in the man's attitude and reception of him as a colleague. This man could be racist against me Alpha thought, even though we were in the same category substitute teachers. But the fact that the Latino man had a fairer color that was more acceptable to the whites and so he was on the advantage side of things. He was more welcomed by the whites than Alpha and so he was a lot closer to them. They befriended him and he was assured of a regular job at the end of the first year.

Next day was Friday; Alpha came into the room and found only four text books in the room. He asked the Head of department for more books. Alpha was told that there were enough text books for all the students in the room.

Mr. Alpha asked the transformed man, from a more lucrative and better paid professional job to become a teacher on arrival in the United States from Macao. The man told Alpha that he had no idea what happened to the text books. He shared the room with Alpha and he was using the same textbooks for his groups and he also used the room as Homeroom. Mr. Alpha talked to the head of department about the books before he went home. He found a few textbooks in the room the next day after he told Alpha that he had no idea where they were.

One morning Alpha tried to use the OHP and the bulb blew up. This adopted Doctor teacher made an issue out of that. He tried to smear Alpha by brewing a hurricane in a tea cup to get Alpha out of the room and out of the building.

He told every teacher in the department especially the white teachers and those that spoke his mother tongue and friends and the assistant Principal how Alpha let his students spoil the OHP which he needed for his own classes. He went to the office and complained to the principal.

He brought the assistant principal to show him the damage to the OHP. He alleged that the students in Alpha's class cut the wires in the OHP and had destroyed it completely. Alpha came in and met the man explaining to the assistant principal. But he stopped talking suddenly when Alpha came into the room and Alpha decided to give him the benefit of the doubt and said nothing because he knew that it was just the bulb that blew up. He had never used that AV instrument before so he did not know how it operated.

He was trying to paint a picture of Alpha from his negative attitude towards Alpha and hiding his own ignorance of how the equipment really operated. It was because that was the first time he was in the classroom and he had not used the OHP before as a teaching aid and so he was not aware that the bulb could blow out. But his negative thoughts about Alpha and what he had been saying behind the closed door about Alpha he had tried to put into motion as a smear tactic so that Alpha would be looked at as ineffective and inefficient in his handling of the students.

This man had never been a teacher but because everybody could be a classroom teacher as long as they had right people in the right places and just a degree from any where and in any subject. And so the man was teaching without professional teacher training and every one was happy and he had already been tipped for a regular job. But he did not want to see Alpha because he was black even though he was a trained and qualified teacher in his subject area and Alpha had no connections anywhere and the whites who controlled the steering wheel were shying away from Alpha. The man knew that and he was taking advantage of Alpha's circumstances.

That afternoon Alpha went to Staples store and bought the bulb which blew out. Next morning Alpha fixed the bulb and turned the OHP on.

Alpha told Dr. Ovamboland that he had replaced the bulb that blew out. "Was it working?" Dr. Ovamboland asked with a surprised voice. He went and tried out the OHP and the light came on and he smiled. "How much did the bulb cost?" he asked Alpha.

"Not a lot" Alpha replied.

"I would give you the money back" he told Alpha in a friendly tone.

"Did not worry about it" Alpha replied with a negative body language.

Alpha had to fix a lock to store his stationary. His pencils and papers disappeared the sooner he collected them and put them in the cabinets. His students had no access to any of the cabinets, during his lessons.

The room was also used by Ms Buganda the white female teacher who was very friendly with Ovamboland. She was in the room across the hall but she could not keep anything in her room because the students ruled the room. Ms Buganda came to the room repeatedly each lesson. Ms Buganda was in room 617, but came over three or more times each lesson to collect items from her cabinet or just to look at what was going on in Alpha's room to gossip with other white folks in the building. Since she was white, she was on the safe zone and she was given a regular job within the school year while Alpha who had all the experience, qualifications was discriminated upon from every angle in the school by any one with a light skin color and even black people with an American accent would not want to talk to him and kept their distance from him. His only friend and compatriot was the African lady next door who knew the system and how to manipulate it to her own advantage. She gave Alpha valuable advice on many things for his own very survival and she was the only one who talked to him. Students had asked him repeatedly if she was his wife or girl friend or something.

One morning, Alpha came late from the Focus room in the ground floor. The assistant principal opened the door. He stood by the door until Alpha came in.

Wilderman Effeyon brought a bottle of shampoo. He sprayed it on the floor all over the back of the room behind the lab tables before Alpha came in. When Alpha entered the classroom and was taking class attendance and at the same time he was trying to get the students settled down to begin the lesson. Wilderman was dancing the reverse Wako Jakko dance at the back of the room. Alpha went up to him to get him to sit down. He slipped and nearly fell. The back of the room was now all wet and slippery.

Mr. Alpha called the Office and the assistant principal came in to take Wilderman away. But Wilderman denied that he sprayed the shampoo in the room since Alpha did not see him spray the shampoo. The room was cleaned up by the cleaners later on.

Alpha had to write Wilderman up every other day, because he brought to class various objects to disrupt the lesson.

Alpha came to know that his mom was a professional in her job and his Dad had a very good job too. But he was the last child in the family, and so they treated him with some specialty. He got away with anything and everything. He was a troublesome student in every class. He was suspended from school nearly every week. One teacher whispered Wilderman's behavior into Alpha's ear every day since he had him in his classroom first period each morning.

"Wilderman was a pain in my ass every day in my math class." he would start the disruption each time. "He came to my class with an attitude each morning and when you talk to him, he would explode, kicking things, pushing chairs, tables, and swearing. He said Alpha picked on him every day in class but he did not do any class work, he never did homework, he would not cooperate and he would not stop talking. He brought in a walkman into class each morning.

The school rule was that students should not have a walkman in school. But you saw students with walkman in the corridors all the time. The Administrators saw them with a walkman, but turned a blind eye to it. You could not complain, because that will be insubordination. We had to shut up because we wanted our jobs" the man would say to Alpha.

One morning Alpha was in the Focus room and Gill Dumba walked in. He was tall and weighed about 250 pounds. My black brother "Mr. Alpha were you an African? I am certainly an African too. My parents came from Nigeria"

"That was good indeed" Alpha replied. "How much did you know about Nigeria" he would ask Gill.

"Not a lot, I only knew that I am a Yoruba" he replied with a proud voice.

"Did you know which part of Nigeria you find the Yoruba people?"

"No, I did not know" he replied.

"Could you speak Yoruba? Alpha asked him again. "No, but my parents spoke Yoruba."

"Have you been to Nigeria?"

"No, but my dad went two years ago. I knew that Nigeria was a big country and they spoke many languages there."

"Well, I knew a bit about Nigeria. The population was over one hundred million; there were three major ethnic groups, the Yoruba, Hashua and Ibos. They spoke more than two hundred languages in Nigeria."

"Wow that was a lot. I knew there was a lot of oil in Nigeria.

The door opened, and Mr. Flung came in. Alpha got up and left. He looked at his watch. "I had ten minutes to get up to my classroom" he told himself. He walked into the boys' bathroom first, and then he went up the stair to the third floor.

He got to the door, as Dr. Ovamboland normally called Mr. Ovamboland was closing the door to leave. Greg came in to class with an attitude. He kicked his desk, tore the large display papers on the wall. He pulled down the large display of the periodic table.

At the end of the class, Dr Ovamboland Came in and Alpha told him that Greg tore the wall papers and pulled them down. Dr. Ovamboland was full of fury "why did he pull them down. They were high enough. Why did he pull them down?" He asked with an angry voice.

"He came in with an attitude and started pulling things down.

Dr. Ovamboland looked at him with angry looks.

Greg got up. "I did not care, fuck you. Who did you think you were to tell me nonsense" he said with his hands in the air.

"This was my property. I paid for it out of my pocket" he said angrily.

"To hell with you I did not care. I did not want to know in fact I was not going to hang them again. I wanted to see what you could do about it, silly burger."

That was a rude behavior, to pull down my class work. Why didn't you behave yourself? If you had a problem, go and discuss it with someone. You should not come and vent your anger at my teaching aids." He said in an angry voice.

"I did not care if you call yourself Doctor my foot, you should be in a better place than in here. Good doctors work in their proper places and not substitute teachers" Greg said as he got up and walked out of the room through the back door shouting and swearing.

"Mr Alpha, give him an "F" and he would be in my class next year. I would then deal with him." said Dr. Ovamboland in an angry voice.

He was not doing well, actually" Alpha replied calmly. "He came to class each day with an attitude and did not do any class work. He had an abnormal behavior, and he was always looking out for confrontations, so that he could off load his anger and frustrations."

"Did he use drugs?" Dr. Ovamboland asked

"I was not sure" Alpha replied. "But his behavior was just like one. I doubted it if he really knew what he was doing" Alpha went on.

Alpha was cleaning the cabinets when he found the teacher's manual hidden under a pile of student work. Alpha pulled out the book, held it for a while, and shook his head.

He had no home room assignment he had three classes of regular students and one of students thought to be advanced by classification. His first class was made of students with a variety of abilities, including inclusion students, with a variety of mental and behavioral problems.

Some of the students in this special group had unpredictable behavior and he expected anything from complete disaster for the whole period to a calm and friendly atmosphere when these students remember to take their drugs before coming to school.

It was a blue day, and he spent the first two periods in the Focus room. Alpha had the third period in the far end of the building on the third floor. He got to class up there from the basement in the opposite side of the building breathless each time. They refused to give him an elevator key, because he was a substitute. He complained to Mr. Hansue the Principal, who told Alpha that that was good exercise for him. "How could the Principal tell me that, when he knew that I was not quite well.

The head of department Mr. Dwanteh tried to get him out of the focus room to join the rest of the team in the first period each day as planning period. But the Principal put his foot down and said no. Mr. Dwanteh took the matter all the way to the Superintendent, but the Principal would not change his mind and he had the final say about the staff in his school and what they did and what they could not do.

Alpha was now in the black book of the school administrators which was not good for him, as a substitute and a Blackman with an accent which only added fuel to an already bad situation for him.

Alpha now had more eyes watching him from the side lines without him knowing it and the eventual out come which would never be in his favor. A black substitute teacher with no say and no rights in any matter in the school and the principal or his assistants could have him removed out of the school with just a phone call.

Alpha did not get the escalator key, and so he had to climb a hundred and two stairs each day and then a long corridor more than two hundred yards to get to his second period in four minutes.

Alpha got to class almost late each day and breathless, he complained to one of the assistant principals who also told him yet again that, using the stairs was good for his health. The assistant principal could not go against his boss's statement and so Alpha understood the politic of the school.

Alpha had problems with some of his students in one group which he had each morning. Three of the male students in the class who were white and the only whites never wanted to sit still. They wanted to talk to every girl passing by in the corridor. They were always looking out of the door all the time distracting the class. Each time Alpha closed the back door one of the boys would open it, and sneaked out.

The class was full of disruptive students with low IQ, behavior problems, attention deficit and various other problems. He had problems with these students each day and it made life for him like a visit to hell every day.

Alpha had a rough day each and every day with the same students and the same behavior, and writing them up each day never made any difference since they were white and their referrals would not be attended to by the white assistant principals.

One afternoon, Sandy one of the best girls in class who did all her work quietly each day, came in with a work man. Alpha went up to her and told her quietly to put it away. He went back to his desk. One big boy shouted from the back "Why would she have a workman in class and you would not let us use ours?" Alpha called sandy to put her walkman away. She flipped, threw her textbook across the desk, flung her work paper into the air. She swore, cursed and pushed her desk and chair over.

Alpha called for help and she was taken away. Alpha later learned that she had a fight in another room earlier on in the morning and a second fight in the cafeteria. She was to be suspended the next day, because her behavior was getting generally worse by the day.

Two days later, she came back a changed student. She no longer did class work, but looking out for confrontation with the teacher, or other students. Sandy now got suspended every other week or went down to focus room.

She disappeared from class for two weeks in a row. One morning she came to see Alpha during Homeroom time and asked him for her grade in class. "I was moving to another school" she told him. Mr. Alpha gave her the grade she had which was a "B" grade. But he discovered much later on that it had been changed to "F" within the system. This was not unusual, he told himself. He remembered being told by Ms Constantino the Guidance Counselor that the girl in his class was an "A" student according to the school records

But this was a student who was not only irregular in class attendance but hardly did any class work or homework but she was quiet in class and respectful of the teachers. Alpha told her that this girl was working below class average and she could not get an "A" in his subject.

Mr. Alpha this girl was an "A" grade student, you considered that" she said in a commanding voice and she walked away

"I could not give her an "A" grade for doing nothing in my class" he told her. But since Ms Constantino insisted that she was an "A" student, Alpha was in two minds, to do as told and to disobey and got himself into the black book of the school administrators that could land him in rough waters. "I could not give a grade that the student did not deserve" he told himself but after words he had a good thought about it. I would consider the suggestion of the administrator to save my neck and my job.

And this was in support of the other side of his brain that told him to follow instructions, considering his status in the school. The fact that he was black and he was dealing with a white administrator who could destroy his career behind closed doors without him knowing about it. And even if he got to know about it later on he would have nothing to do about it since he was a black sheep and just a substitute teacher for that matter.

At the end of the school year the "D" grade he gave her was changed to "A". It was too late for him to do anything about it when Alpha found out about the grade and he could dare not challenge the white administrator by any means a no go area for a black man.

Alpha was given the usual excuse that mistakes were made in the records office downtown by the computers. Even though all the grades were scrutinized in the school by the guidance office before they were forwarded to the records office.

One afternoon, Alpha was in the shopping mall, one female student who was fun of him in school, she used to help him put things in order and always did her work well and on time, came up to him.

"Mr. Alpha why did you give me an "F" grade?" she asked in front of her relatives. You said in class that I was the best student and yet you gave me an "F" and those who had "Fs" and "Es" got "As" and "B."

This was a hard bone to chew. He had no explanation to give, because she was with her relatives, mother and sisters in a public place away from the school. "That could not be" he told her.

Her mother nodded yes.

"I honestly did not know what happened" he said quietly. Alpha went home and checked his records. The girl had an "A" grade in his mark book.

One Thursday morning Alpha came to class breathless. Gregory came in with a big radio cassette dancing to loud music. He put the set on his desk; put his foot on the desk as well. Alpha came up to him. "Turn off this radio and put your foot down as well.

"No sir, I wanted to listen to the music. I was not in the mode to do any class work today. I just wanted you to leave me alone. You did not have to teach me today" he said in a loud voice.

"Well, if you did not turn this radio off and put it away, I would call and have it taken away from you." Alpha said in a stern language.

"Alright, I would leave I hated this fuckin school anyway. There were too many rules which teachers turned a blind eye to for the students they liked. He got up reluctantly and walked out, with the radio set on his shoulder and the music blasting out. Alpha closed the door and went to his desk.

"Why did you give us work every day? you should give us a break you know as other teachers did. It's only you that give us lots of work each day" complained Ashley.

"I hated this class because there was too much work to do. You never got a breathing space. You were not supposed to give work each day, you know" added Felix.

"Who told you that I should give you a break from class work every other day? Alpha asked.

Mr Carr gave us the same work every day for one whole week. As long as you sat down and you did not talk aloud he gave us credit for being good students in his class. I did not know what we were doing in his class room, because I never open the text book, but I got a "B" grade in his class.

Alpha remembered being told by a veteran teacher one lunch break that "these students were not supposed to learn anything as the hidden curriculum."

It was a white day Alpha had a double class in room 6249 with a variety of students both in ability and behavior. The white students made up the minority in the class. They sat together in the back of the class. These were low IQ students, but because they were white, they were put in the advanced class. They did not like Alpha personally being black teacher and a substitute with an accent. They did things to slow the progress of the lesson. They would talk, play cards which they knew was not permitted to do, made odd sounds, while Alpha was explaining procedures to the class.

Sometimes they looked for confrontations with Alpha so that they could make racist comment about Alpha; they made rude remarks, or made statements that would hurt Alpha's feelings.

He wrote them up repeatedly, but nothing got better. They would lash at Alpha with nasty words, knowing that nothing was going to happen, because all the principals and Administration were all white and he Alpha was the only black African and a substitute for that matter. Sometimes they made derogatory remarks, referring to his race.

One day one of the boys asked Alpha if his anus was black, and if his wife had a good smell. Alpha was very upset, but he controlled his anger. One of the very vocal black boys got up to go and fight with the white boy. Alpha told him not to fight. "I am very upset. How could you let these bastards talk to you like that? We could not sit down and have these boys talk to you like that and use all those nasty words on you and did nothing about it.

I knew you could not do anything about it because you were not supposed to. You wrote them up and give to Mr. Helsinki, he would do nothing about it, because he was white and these boys were all white."

The boy knew that Tyrone was going to beat him up, he ran out of the room.

The bell rang, all the boys left. The girls stayed to talk to Alpha.

"Mr. Alpha what were you going to do about these boys? They were very rude to you, and they had no respect for you. We were not happy the way they talked to. The whites who controlled the school would not do anything about it. They would believe what these white boys told them about you. You were to soft on these white boys." The girls left because the next class was coming in.

The next day Alpha stood by the door waiting for the students to come in. Keith came in, stood by Alpha, and looked into Alpha's eyes. "I hated you

Blackie, you go back to the zoo in Africa. By the way where was your green card?"

I told the Principal that you were not a good teacher you should go and teach in Africa" he walked to his seat.

Alpha wrote up the boys the other day, but he came back to class. Nothing had been done about what he said the previous day.

Phyllis and Danny came late to class each day. They came through the back door and walked to their seats. The trio sat down talking, while Alpha was teaching. "Keep quiet boys and listen" he told them.

"I did not want to listen to you. I was not interested in what you were saying" Phyllis replied.

"Well, for the benefit of those who wanted to listen and were interested in getting good grades for the course, you had to be quiet. "I would be getting a good grade for this course with or without you anyway, your grade was not important," replied Danny in a rude and raised voice. The trio laughed they knew that they would be given good grades by the administration in the guidance office and so teachers grades did not matter as white students and the head of the section was a white woman.

As the rest of the class was working quietly, Alpha went up to them. "Look here guys if you needed help, you simply call me. I would come over and give you help he told them quietly.

"I have no textbook stormed Phyllis. I did not understand what you were saying. You were not a good teacher. You did not explain properly what you wanted us to do." He got up pushed his desk, kicked his chair.

"He was telling a lie" shouted Wendy. He had a text book when Ms Fish was here, and he was not behaving like that, because the woman was a bitch like him.

"You shut up. I was not talking to you"

Tom got up."If you say one more word to her I will kick your ass. Just one more word" Tom said angrily.

Phyllis stopped talking. He got up and walked out of the room through the back door.

At the end of the period, Alpha went to see Mrs. DeCastillo, the head of the advanced placement school. He explained to her what had happened and what these three boys had been doing in class.

"Phyllis was here, he told me what happened. Mr. Alpha, you should know that Phyllis, and Danny were special education Students.

They were IEP students, with behavioral problems. Phyllis came to us from another school. We decided to put him in this class for special reasons" she said calmly. This was news to me; I have never been told that these students were special education students.

This was the policy of the district to give information about certain students only to some teachers and not to all and to pass certain information about some students from one teacher to teacher via cliques, whispers and casual discussions between close friends, making it difficult for those who did not know how to deal with certain situations in the classroom when they occurred. By not knowing that certain students had behavioral problems or special medical conditions, teachers tended to treat all the students in the same way, resulting in unwanted outcomes in extreme situations in the name of privacy laws.

"Keith told me the other day that I bought my certificates, and that I should tell him where I bought them so that he could go and buy his.

Mrs. DeCastillo said nothing. She simply got up and left the room without saying a word to Alpha, an indication that she accepted the students' explanations, because Alpha was a black teacher and a substitute. She did not do or said anything about the complaint Alpha told her about what the boy said about his wife. Alpha got up and went down to the teachers' room. He looked upset as he entered the room. One of the African –American veteran teachers asked Alpha what happened. Alpha told him what the boys said to him and he told the head of the advanced placement school. That she did not say a word and she walked out of the room leaving Alpha in the room, an indication that all what the students said to Alpha about his black anus and his wife being smelly were not important to her and she believed in what the white students said to her.

Nothing ever happened and the write ups were probably thrown into the garbage as not worth acting on.

Mr. Daniel told Alpha that anything a white student told a white administrator about you the black teacher was accepted as the whole truth. You were in a bad position he told Alpha, being a substitute teacher and being black the principal of the section of the school would not take your words seriously.

I could go and speak my mind to her about what I felt about her and her administration, but you could not because you were a substitute teacher they could have you replaced just like that and you needed to work every day to get the money you needed to look after your family.

We had a big problem in our hands as black people. You see the Principal of this school since he was black, all the whites in this building were in a league to sabotage his administration and bring him down. They were doing everything to discredit him and made him looked like being inefficient and got him out of here.

It was Wednesday afternoon when Alpha had the same class. The class was working quietly, when Keith came in noisily without a late pass. .He came through the back door as usual. Danny went to open the door for him. He screamed very loudly as he walked to his seat. "Keith, you came in very late, without a pass and you were now disrupting the class. Would you keep quiet please" Alpha said to him quietly.

"I would do what I felt like, you did not tell me what I had to do, because I did not listen to you" he replied in a loud noisy voice.

"You had two choices, either you sat down and kept quiet or you went out of the room and straight to the assistant principal's office.

You already had a detention for coming late without a late pass.

"Detention in your ass" he shouted. I would never do a detention for you black Monkey.

Alpha came up to him "go outside now" he commanded.

"I was not going anywhere Mr. Blackie" he replied sitting down.

"Were you going outside or not? Alpha asked in a raised and commanding voice.

"No" he replied sharply.

Alpha walked to the phone to call Mr. Fitzgerald the assistant Principal.

Keith got up walked to the back door "Bitch, black bastard. He opened the door walked out and banged it with a loud noise

Alpha wrote the disciplinary referral. He went back to Mrs. DeCastillo, told her what happened.

"You wrote a report for him?" she asked. "Yes" Alpha replied.

"If he made a racial remark that was what would be taken care of." she assured him.

Alpha took the referral to the assistant principal's office on the second floor. He explained to the secretary who was white what happened and left. One week passed, nothing happened.

Friday morning, Keith met Alpha on the corridor. "You kept writing me up. You were wasting your time. Mr. Helsinki would not look at it Blackie. Go back to the zoo."

Alpha complained to the head of department, in the presence of two other white folks.

"Was this the white boy in your class? asked Mr. Carr. "Yes" Alpha replied

"No wonder, I could see where this was coming from" he said in a disappointing voice.

"I could not do anything for you; go to Mr. Helsinki the assistant principal. He could take action." said Mr. Carr.

"But you knew how the system worked here? said Mr. Carr. More than ninety percent of the referrals were not dealt with. I had decided not to write any more referrals, because it was a waste of your time."

Alpha complained to other teachers.

It was Wednesday of the third week and it was lunch time in the morning. Alpha was going to the teachers' room for lunch when Mr. Peters stopped him. "I heard that a white boy called you black bastard? He asked.

"Yes" Alpha replied.

"What did you do about it?" he asked Alpha in an angry voice.

"I wrote a referral and complained, but nothing had been done about it."

"I was going now to confront Mr. Helsinki about it I would not take that. If that was me, they would find the boy on the floor half dead." He went back into his room with angry steps

Next morning Alpha was in the Focus room in the first period as usual. In came Mr. Helsinki, with a thick pile of referrals in his hands. "Mr. Peter came and told me that a boy made a racial remark at you and I did not do anything about it. You see how many referrals I have to deal with each day even though it was already three weeks when Alpha handed in the referral.

It was obvious that the student knew about the write up and had spoken to Alpha about that particular referral, who could have told him about that referral besides Mr. Helsinki himself? The principal was pretending with an excuse three weeks later when referrals were dealt with within two days and not three weeks.

He must have removed that write up from the discard box to pretend to be dealing with it soon. Alpha knew that it was an excuse he was making but he said nothing being that he was on the receiving end with all the disadvantages around him and the favoritism that was going around for both white students and teachers.

Your write up was right at the bottom of the pile. He talked to me as if I was condoning student disrespect of teachers. If there was any urgent matter, you needed to talk to me direct about it, before you complain to other teachers," he said in a mixed voice signal

Yesterday morning, Mr. Peter came to me he said he heard that one student called me black bastard and what did I do about it. I told him that I wrote the boy up and took it to your office, but you were not there but I explained the incident to the secretary before I gave her the referral. He had a call on the intercom and he left in a hurry.

Later in the day, Alpha was in the Cafeteria doing teachers duty when Mr. Helsinki approached him again. "I have suspended the boy I told him that you wanted to talk to his mom before he could come back to your class. But I was not sure if his mother would come to see you. She said she would not come, because she had just started a new job and would not be able to take a day off to come to school." he walked off. Alpha knew that he was making an excuse for the boy's parent yet again because she would not come to talk to a black man for her son.

Next morning Alpha was in Focus room. Mr. Helsinki came in again. "Could I talk you Alpha?"

They went outside the room. "I had thought of a punishment for Keith. He was going to do an internet research on your country in Africa. He needed to learn something about your home country. He would write it up and bring it to you to read it and approved it before he would come back to school. How about that?

He looked into Alpha's eyes. "That was alright it sounded to me." Alpha replied with mixed emotion.

"If that was OK with you I would let him start the research." He left without another word. The student was in school even though Mr. Helsinki the assistant principal said he had suspended him from school.

Next day Keith came back to class early. He did not say a word to Alpha, nor mentioned anything about the research.

Nobody said anything to Alpha. The matter seemed closed. Keith remained silent for the rest of the period, because his two white friends were both absent from school that day

Next day Keith Came to class early. Mr. Alpha could I do my class work in Ms Door's room?" he asked quietly.

"Yes of course" Alpha replied. He explained to him the exercises and gave him some papers to write on.

Ms Door was a white teacher up the corridor. Keith left before the rest of the class came in.

He came back towards the end of the class, gave in his work and left.

The three boys kept to themselves at the back of the room. The rest of the class were Black and Hispanic students. They did not want to have anything to do with the "white boys" as they called them.

One afternoon, in the second half of the two period's class, Brandon was talking, and Danny interrupted him rudely. Brandon got up, went and swept Danny to the floor. Alpha went and separated them. "You think I was Mr. Alpha who you tell all nasty thing, and garbage talk and nobody was doing anything about it because the assistant principal was white like you. I would beat the hell out of you nasty smelly idiot.

Danny said not a word; he simply walked out of the class, because Brandon was the tallest and biggest boy in the class. He was nearly twice the height of Danny, and could lift Danny by the ears.

The rest of the class applauded Brandon. "That was what these white scums deserved" said Hify.

Mr. Alpha you leave these white asses to us to deal with them. They were all wind bags, and nothing else. We would keep them under control. Any one who talked garbage to you now, would get a slap on his face. I did not care if I got suspended, but they could not go on disrespecting you all the time" Said Hajj in an angry voice.

Keith and Phyllis got up and left the room without a word.

CHAPTER FIVE

NEXT WEDNESDAY MORNING ALPHA got to this large High school near down town. He was told to take the place of an absent teacher on the second floor. He was in a team with other five teachers. The other Black African-American teacher was open minded.

Each morning Alpha attended a team meeting in the first period. The meetings started in Ms Odooje's room. The meetings were attended by the staff in the team, the professional development coordinator, special needs teacher and the assistant principal Mr. Duartey. The meetings were often marred with arguments about procedures, teacher control issues. It was a professional development meeting with a teacher thought to be the professional development coordinator. But these meetings never produce any things other than arguments, led by the Alpha male who was the cock of the group and who had been in the school for so long that he thought he was the Bible and Mr knew it all in the school and the team. These meetings were no more than a school politics public relationships with the unions. No serious issue was ever discussed and there had never been any item on any agenda that teachers had an accord. It was nothing more than a debating forum with no specific issue and no agreement on any item and all the meetings ended abruptly on the sound of the bell. The lead teacher was not only ineffective but she had no idea on how to conduct meetings, managed people and it was like free for all agenda. One often wondered what was the purpose of those meetings and what they hoped to achieve in the end since no item was resolved except read loud in class that seemed to be her one and only emphasis at every meeting.

The principal attended one meeting in which he said teachers would be paid even if they did not achieve their intended teaching target. But that he would like each teacher to try something new each day.

He said more than half of the students in the school were failing last year. He wanted teachers to improve their teaching methods so that more students would achieve and meet the state standards. Lots of emphasis was placed on reading aloud in class.

Alpha thought that the emphasis placed on reading aloud in class in the high school seemed a misplaced priority.

Reading was part and parcel of education from day one in the school more so in the elementary school. The fact that student went to school year in year out without reading anything had resulted into an army of defective and deficient reading generation of students in the school system. What should have been emphasized in the first few years of a child's education was now the emphasis in the high school.

If students went to school up to high school and they had not been motivated to read anything, the writer doubted very much how reading aloud in high school would yield the results intended in the curriculum.

One of the teachers in the team was very vocal on the issue of reading aloud and would want to see how reading aloud would have positive effects in the teaching of mathematics, because all the text books in use were written in English. If not only some students but most of the students could not read which was a basic fact of the solution as it existed but nobody would accept that fact. How would they be able to understand and solve simple problems in mathematics. There was never a simple and direct answer and even the so called professional development coordinator could not answer this simple logical riddle.

The exercise was more or less a marking time and a forum to bring team teachers together for open discussion that had no real academic value and certainly would not improve teaching methods and students' output in state examinations.

Alpha was looked upon as a black person by his white colleagues. Differences in behavior began to emerge, Mr. Hoof the cock of the team and the spokes man and team leader and oldest teacher in the school stopped visiting Alpha's room each morning.

The inclusion teacher stopped coming to Alpha's room, even though Alpha had five inclusion students in each group.

The class assistant too, a Liberian man who accompanied one of the students to class, stopped coming'

Alpha tried to exert control in his classes, but the students were lazy, uncooperative and very disruptive.

Fissy an IEP student, never came prepared to class. He would not stop talking; and he would not sit still for a few minutes. He did not following directions, he went round the room disrupting other students. He had problem sitting down still for a short time. He was all over the place, and loved to play with girls hairs. He was always in the company of other IEP girls.

One Fridays, the team discussed student work and behavior. Fissy was always the subject of discussion. The class room assistant who accompanied Fissy urged that he be put in a self contained room with other students with similar behavior. "Fissy's behavior was such that he disrupted the learning of other students and the teacher's lesson in general" he said. But because of cut backs on teacher numbers and financial constraints, the idea was not even considered to put him in an environment suitable for his behavior.

No meeting ever came to a conclusion or any idea adequately discussed.

The arguments would drag on to the end of the period. The meetings were more of debating sessions, than professional development and were dominated by one person all the time.

One Monday morning, Ms Odoojie gave a three hole punch to Alpha. "Thanks very much. How much did it cost?" he asked "Its $23" she replied.

Alpha reached his wallet to pull out the money to pay so that the punch would be his. Ms Odoojie walked away. "I have the money here" he told her.

"Did not worry about it, it was for your use" she said without turning round.

Alpha had a difficult time with period three. Alloy who dressed and looked very much like a girl sometimes befriended Alpha and at other times he was a real pain in class He would stay after school to work on the computer in the room. One morning he came to see Alpha and pretended to be a good boy in the home room period. He brought a packet of tooth picks; he threw them around as soon as Alpha turned round to write on the board. Alpha took the box from him and gave him class detention which he did not do. Alpha wrote him up and gave the referral to the assistant Principal but no action was taken.

Next day, Alloy brought pastas and he was throwing them around the room as soon as Alpha turned round to write on the board again. Some of the students complained about the pastas. Alloy hid them in his book bag. Alpha went to the far end of the room to help a girl. Alloy threw a hand full of the pastas on the floor. Gary did not know that they were slippery. He nearly fell over when he stepped on one of them.

Alpha went to Alloy and explained to him that if a student fell over and broke a bone over the pastas he was throwing around, his parents would be in serious trouble.

"I did not do anything" he stormed. "What have I done, why were you picking on me? I had nothing with me" he got up threw the rest of the pastas on the floor. "You hated me, and you did not like me. I did not like you either"

"Mr. Alpha, he wanted you to fall and hurt yourself on the pastas" shouted Bianca.

"You pick them up" Alpha said in a commanding voice. "I would write you up, if you did not pick them up."

"I did not care, you could write me up." The bell rang, and Alloy turned the whole box on the floor and left.

Alpha wrote him up. But nothing was done about it because he was white and all the school administrators were white and he the teacher was black and a substitute teacher.

Next day, Alloy came to class, sat down quietly and did all his work. "Mr. Alpha could I come after school today and work on the computer?" he asked politely.

Alpha discovered that the internet cable had been removed and the computer was no longer working, even though Alloy worked on it' the previous afternoon. He tried to find out the fault, but he could not. He called Ms. Odoojie for help. She brought one of her students to fix the fault. The girl tried, but did not find the fault, and left.

It was the fourth period which was lunch time. All the students were outside the building talking and socializing. The group in class was made of lazy IEP students who were not motivated to do any work. They would rather look through the window down the large pavement where most of the students were.

The Principal was outside with the students. He saw two students by the window looking out. He called the office to tell Alpha to get the students off the window. Alpha told the secretary that the students had gone to their seats.

The Principal came up and went over to Alpha's room. "I saw the students over your window and called the secretary to tell you to get the students away from the window. You could not tell me that I did not see the students by the window" he said with an angry voice. His voice and posture and body language were those of a man giving instructions to his servant or worst his slave in a disrespectful language in front of the students. He walked out with angry steps, bang the door behind him.

"Mr. Alpha, these people have too much power. All the teachers were afraid of him, you know. He had a dirty mouth with the teachers. He talked down on everyone in the school. He was just a proud person?"

"No he was not" shouted André. "Why did you not answer him back? he had no respect for you."

"He should not talk to you like that" said Gail in the back seat.

"He was the Principal, he could fire Mr. Alpha from the school" said Johnny. "He was conscious of his position as principal of the school, that was it he had all the power and he could punish any teacher in the school and nobody would say a word about it. Every teacher in here was like a servant to him, if you were not his personal friend. He had respect for only those who could talk back to him like his friends."

"I thought they gave too much power to these people. But I did not care, how much power he had, if he talked to me like that, I would answer back. All he would do was suspend me for three days. I would have said what I wanted to say to him any way" said Andree.

It was Wednesday morning when Alloy brought a toy machine that made audible noises. He kept it in his book bag. Each time Alpha was not looking at him, he set the toy off quickly.

"Alloy, you turned off that toy and put it away or you give it to me." Alpha told him, as the students laughed.

"I did not have anything" he replied. "I did not have anything Mr. Alpha" He opened his hands swung them around. Every one laughed, including himself.

Alpha sent him out, he refused to go out. Alpha called the Office for the administrator to come get him out of the class and then he turned the toy fully on as he walked slowly towards the door. Mr. Dwartie came in as Alloy was by the door when Mr. Dwartie opened it from outside. "You write him up and send it to me" he told Alpha.

"This was a problem class" he remarked before he left.

Alloy came in after school to use the computer. He sat quietly by the computer

It was Tuesday morning. Alpha went to attend the professional development meeting. "I had got some reading material "he told Ms. Lauro the professional development coordinator. But I was not sure if it was too difficult" he went on.

"I would have a look at them tonight" she told Alpha in a dismissive voice.

The meeting did not go on well, as usual.

The theme was reading aloud which the school had put lots of emphasis on for the whole school and for the year round to improve students work attitudes. "I had a problem how you would design a reading lesson in mathematics. Mathematics was not a reading subject. So I found it rather difficult to live up to the school expectations on the reading program" said Mr. Bean the mathematics teacher.

"I would look up for some materials that would be appropriate for your math subject" Ms Lauro assured Mr. Bean.

Alpha discovered that Ms Odoojie was paying particular attention to him and his work. It was a mixed reception. On the one hand, he thought that being black; she was spying on him as was always the case being black in a white institution. You stood out quite distinctly among the faculty. She was trying to find out what he was doing and how well he was doing his work. The attitude towards black people that they had to work twice as hard to attain the minimum standard of the white colleague was quite evident.

The other thought that came to him though not quite strongly was that she was interested in him after all thinking that Alpha was not married.

Alpha decided to carry on his classroom duties as usual, without taking any notice of her and what she was up to.

At the end of each period the teachers stood outside their door to usher the students into their room. Sometimes Ms Odoojie came over and said a word or two to Alpha and cracked a joke with a smile which Alpha thought was false.

It was one Wednesday afternoon Alpha was in the teachers' room, also used as copy room. He sat in the settee in the middle of the room, reading his news paper. There were other teachers in the room, some eating their lunch on the table near the wall, others just talking and doing some corrections. The cock of the group came in talking on top of his voice. Ms Odoojie came in minutes later and sat opposite Alpha.

She looked at Mr Hoof, then at Alpha. "Well, we have not had an opportunity to talk to Alpha yet" she said. "Tell us about your family life. Alpha told them he got married recently, had three grown up children, all at University and two little kids at home. Ms. Odoojie got up and left without saying a word walked away into her room.

Alpha completed the photocopying and returned to his room.

Next morning, Alpha discovered that Ms. Odoojie's attitude towards him had changed towards negativity. She would not smile to him any more, nor wanted to talk to him again. Each time Alpha went to talk to her or to ask for something, she appeared to be busy and reluctant to talk to him.

Mr Hoof's attitude had also changed for the worst.

Alpha locked himself out of his room one afternoon and he went to Mr. Hoof who was the only teacher around with the key to open the door for him. "You must be really stupid to have locked yourself out. You better get a key from someone else. I did not know where my keys were" he told Alpha in a disgusting voice, and walked away to the far end of the corridor.

Alpha stood there like a fool, trying to think what to do next and who to approach for the room key.

He watched Mr. Hoof who walked on but kept looking back at Alpha.

Then Alpha decided to walk into Gary's room and asked him for the key to open his door. Gary gave him the keys.

The next morning, Alpha came to school early. He opened the door and saw Ms Odoojie and Mr. Hoof talking in the teachers' room. He went up to them to join in their conversation they stopped talking, and went in opposite directions. Mr. Hoof walked a few steps, turned round and went into his room. "Why would these folks behaved like that? Was it because I was black" he asked himself. Alpha did not discuss the incident with Gary, the two white guys in the team kept at arms length from Alpha there after. They no longer told him what was going on in the team. He now only got information from Gary.

On Friday, they discussed student affairs. His contributions and concerns were no longer seen as important.

The usual communications between team members had come to a dead end and Alpha now felt isolated and no longer a member of the team. The team members usually met at Ms. Odoojie's room for lunch. Neither Alpha, nor Gary joined the lunch time meeting again.

One afternoon, Alpha decided to walk into Ms. Odoojie's room just to test the waters. They were talking joyously with loud laughers. But the minute Alpha came in, the atmosphere changed to a somber mode. They were all pretending to be busy eating. Alpha knew that he was not welcomed. He walked out without saying a word. He went into the teachers' room which was just opposite Ms Odoojie's room. There was an out bust of laughter after he left the room and he could observe the reaction of the teachers from the teachers room. The atmosphere had again become buoyant with laughter and loud talking the sooner he walked out of the room.

Mr. Alpha went into his room, through the back door. He closed the door behind him. He sat down looked out of the window into the sky. He could see black clouds drifting across his vision and the words "that was it"

This was not what should happen, but this was the reality of the situation. Alpha was in his room and he over heard Mr. Hoof saying that he had a meeting with Nabisco the assistant Principal to discuss some urgent developments.

It was Friday afternoon Alpha decided to take home his files and personal stationary which he brought from his home. "I would take these, just in case I was told to go to another school next Monday.

It was Monday morning, Alpha just got up and as he would have it the call came in at 7.10 he was told to go back to the school. He got there, but they did not need him. He was sent back to the main building. He was going towards the main Office when he saw Ms. Odoojie and Mr Hoof going to the Principal's Office. "Oh, there he was again. He was back" said Mr. Hoof. They both disappeared into the Principal's Office.

Alpha went to see the principal who told him to go upstairs and hand over the key, the mark book and tell the teacher where the books were. Alpha went upstairs reluctantly. Some of the students expressed disappointment and some had mixed feelings. Alpha spent the day in the first floor.

CHAPTER SIX

Tuesday morning Alpha was told to go to Howard Middle School. He was happy that he was on the trail again. He was told it was a two day assignment which later turned out to be an endless assignment. He got to school and was told to go room 601. He was walking along the corridor when one teacher stopped him "Were you going into that room?" he asked Alpha. "Yes" he replied. There were very bad classes in that room, you have to be very strong indeed, he warned.

"Oh God here I go again. I thought I was having a break." he told himself.

Alpha had been in this room before, with the same students.

The note the teacher left for the substitute was vague and terrifying. "You could do what you wanted to do with the students. But pay a particular attention to period 4, some students would throw anything through the window. Keep them away from the windows, good luck."

Alpha had mixed reception as was always the case with a teacher returning to a class room after a while. Some students were happy, jubilant and welcoming; some came to shake hands with him warmly.

"Why did you leave us in the first place? Why did you not come back soon? Have you come back for ever?" were some of the questions some students asked, some others were negative about his return. "Were you going to be our teacher forever? Oh God help me please."

Some students showed surprised faces and mixed emotions at seeing Alpha again.

Alpha went to sit down after reading the note left on the desk for him he looked at the text books left on the table, then opened to the chapter the students could do. Every page in the book had been turn in the middle into two halves. Alpha shook his head and decided to look at all the text books under the students desks. They were all in the same condition. Some in fact were in worst condition, no cover, several pages were missing in a lot of the textbooks, the glossary was missing in nearly all of the books.

Things had changed not for the better though" he told himself.

It was the beginning of period four. He was getting mentally ready for the most challenging part of the day.

The students came in noisily, some rowdy, some jumping, you name it. The assistant principal who was in his room next door came out and screamed. There was temporal quietness. The group of difficult boys drifted in screaming and shouting. The two oldest seventh graders, Taucose and Anthonia came in last. They rushed to the girls, tried to fumble with them and the girls were running around.

Alpha screamed twice, but the noise was so loud that no one noticed his presence. He went to his desk bang the table several times. The noise was dying out when Taurose ran out of the room into the corridor.

Alpha went out to get him. The noise grew louder again. He took the phone to call for help, there was quiet. He was then able to talk to the class and then explained the assignment, and gave some directions on how to answer the questions. Anmoron went and rubbed off part of the board and ran out of the room. Alpha went out to bring him. The noise again grew louder.

It was time for lunch he took the group to the cafeteria in the basement. He went into the teachers' room briefly, and then went up to the library. He returned to his room. Alpha went down to Mr. Obomba's room in the basement. He received Alpha warmly "I was really fed up and tied" Obomba told him. I could not wait for the end of the school year. This was not a pleasant job" he told Alpha. "You were alright" he told Alpha, since you were already in the last step as a teacher. You just hung in there until you retired."

Monday morning, he was told to go back to the school for the same teacher. But this time he was told to keep going until he was told other wise. He later learnt that four other teachers had left that room and had refused to come back.

The day did not go well as expected.

Next day it was the fourth period, Alpha had to call for help. The assistant Principal Mr. Beneforti came in.

"I was sick of this class. This was the fifth teacher in so many weeks in this room. The last teacher resigned, and told us that he was not ready to deal with your behavior. I expected you to cooperate with Mr. Alpha and gave him a chance to teach those students who wanted to learn. You had to give them a chance to get the education they came to get from the school. Parents of some of you complained that some students disrupt the learning of their kids. The parents had a right to complain and some of you came to school with the wrong attitude."

One of the students said" but Mr Beneforti, he had an accent and he could not speak English."

"Mr Alpha was going to be here until we employed a teacher for you. You just cooperate with him," he replied and left. This was a perfect example that a substitute teacher was not a real teacher and so Alpha was not a teacher by school administrators and students standard in the district.

The substitute teacher syndrome in the American school system was alive.

Each day Alpha had difficulty with all the classes but the worst one was period four, who just came back from the gym and were still full of the exercise energy. Zabeck was the only white boy in a class of 28 he had an erratic behavior and he would stand outside the corridor until some black kid picked on him or hit him. Some times they wrestled him to the floor. He would refuse to come in to class he would stand behind the door until some black student either punched him or pushed him around before he would sit down.

Many times he would bring a dog tape and glued it on the door, so that he would be able to run in and out of the door. Alpha had had to remove this tape many times. He had written him up for it several times, but no action had been taken. Sometimes he brought plastic spoons which he would put between the door lock, so that Alpha would not be able to lock the door and stopped him from running out of the room.

Mr. Alpha had held conferences with Zabeck many times about his behavior without success. If he came into class at all he would refuse to sit down. He would jump and sit on the teacher's desk. Telling him to get up from the table was equal to telling him to leave the room, which he would do immediately. He would be the first student to fold his class work into a plane and throw it around. "White boy, sit down" they called him. He would run around, throw scraps of papers to other students to start a quarrel, or out of the window. Sometimes he brought a large number of plastic spoons and distributed them around to gain recognition from the black boys. At the end of the fourth period, you had a large number of broken spoons around the room.

Alpha had reported this incident to the assistant Principal whose Office was next door, and they share the same phone. Mr. Alpha, Zabeck was behaving like that all the time last year and he behaved like that in other classes too." Elzar told Mr. Alpha.

It was one Wednesday afternoon, when Andy came in late to class he went and sat down in the back row. Alpha was helping some female students in the front row. Andy crawled on his knees, went to Alpha's desk, took one packet Xerox paper and a pencil box he hid them under the TV stand.

Alpha saw him crawling back to his seat. He went to Andy's desk and found one Xerox package and a half box of pencils. He went to his desk and found two Xerox packages missing and all the pencils gone.

He called Andy. "I saw you crawling behind my desk and I found copy papers on your desk and the pencils under your coat on your desk. Where were the rest of the pencils and paper?"

"I did not know. I did not have them" he replied angrily. "Look under the TV" some one shouted. "Why were you stealing the paper and pencils? These were for every one in the class."

"I was not a thief, but I needed the papers for my computer at home. I did not take your pencils" he said in an angry voice.

"What about these I found on your desk" What were they doing there?"

"I did not know who put them there but could I have the paper for my computer, please." he said.

"Bring your book bag let me have a look at it." Alpha demanded.

"No, no way, you have no right to look into my book bag" he stormed. "Fuck you bastard" he walked away.

One of the boys took his book bag brought it and emptied it on the floor. A box of pencils dropped from it.

The boy took the box of pencils and showed it to the class. Every one laughed.

"How did these pencils got into your bag." Alpha asked.

"My mum bought them for me" he replied.

"You liar, we saw you took the pencils and put them into you book bag. That was not all" shouted another student. Alpha went into the side pockets of the bag and found more pencils.

"Those pencils did not belong to you" he said defiantly

"He stole them from Ms Zimm" a girl said at the back.

Where were the rest of the papers?" Alpha asked with fury. "I was going to call the assistant Principal if you did not tell me where the rest of the papers were"

"Have you looked everywhere? They might have fallen some where" he said in a low condescending voice.

"Look here, the papers have no legs to walk about. You got that into your head." Alpha told him in a strong voice.

"Mr. Alpha look under the TV stand," shouted Anna from the central row. Alpha pulled the TV and took the papers and pencils away.

Next day, there was a fight outside the room in the corridor. Alpha went out to stop the fight. When he came back, the papers and pencils on the table had disappeared. Andy sat unconcerned, pretending to be working. Alpha went up to him. "Where were the papers and pencils on the table? Yesterday, I caught you stealing from my cabinets, and today you went back and took the papers from the desk. Take it out now before I call the assistant Principal" he said in a commanding voice.

"I did not have it' he stormed. "Why were you accusing me of stealing from your desk. Why were you picking on me? he shouted.

"Open your book bag let me have a look" Alpha told him.

"No" he said in a loud voice.

"Well then, I was going to call Mr Beneforti. Alpha walked away toward the phone.

"Give the papers before you got into trouble. You would be suspended for stealing." Ben told Andy.

Andy took his bag, opened it reluctantly and took out the package of papers. "But sir, I needed these papers for my computer at home. I have no more paper for the printer and my mom had not bought me some yet.

"Let me have these please. Some of it please" he begged as he stretched his hand.

"You would not have any of it. You should learn to ask and not just help your self without asking.

As time went on nothing ever got better. Two big girls in the fourth period were racist, disruptive and confrontational. They both had the mentality of typical African-Americans, general hatred for African people and other black people. Their hatred of Alpha as African was too intense. They did no work, talk on top of their voices all the time, the usual method of talking by most black kids especially girls which was typical noises you heard on the corridors when these kid walked along in a group. They were always looking for confrontation with Alpha and mouthing at him.

"I hated you, I did not like you, and we had no respect for you they would say.

Alpha had written up the two girls many times, and they had been suspended from school a number of times, but none of that reduced the intensity of their hatred for Alpha.

"Mellie could you stop talking during the lesson and allowed the teacher to explain the lesson to the whole class?" Alpha would say to the girls.

They would reply in a disrespectful tome "you shut up what did you think you were? This was not Africa you could not speak English. You were an idiot you smelt bad.

I had told the Principal about you. She told me that you were not permanent. And that she would get rid of you. I did not care about you, you would soon be leaving anyway" she would dance round and came to Alpha stood close to him" The principal said if you did not leave me alone she would fire you.

The Principal did not like you she said, because you had an accent.

Having an accent in the United State Alpha had learned was generally seen by all Americans as synonymous with illiteracy, stupidity and being out right ignorant.

Alpha wrote the girl up and talk to the assistant principal about the statement the girl made. He denied it "I would not make a statement like that to a student" but said the principal might have made that statement but he was not aware of that. No action was taken.

The next day the girl told him "you were wasting your time writing me up, no one would read your referrals."

The fourth period was all the time a real challenge to Alpha. They made the most noise. Each time he handed in dittos, they would fold them and threw around, and out of the windows. The class was made of mostly black students, except one white boy and most of them had anti school attitude. The class had mostly big boys and girls, most of the were way above average class age, some students in the group had repeated twice, others had been expelled from other schools or had some problems with the police.

Some of the students did no class work, but expected the teacher to give them an "A" grade, some did below minimum work and they expected the highest grade for less than minimum work.

I did some work today and you should give me an "A" grade for my effort, other teachers did that.

"Would you give me an "A" grade if I behaved? Other teachers did give us good grades for good behavior you know "May I see my grade." Eric would ask insolently.

"But you had not been doing any class work and you had not presented any homework so far." Alpha would say in a calm voice.

"And so you were not giving me a grade for coming to class every day, as other teachers did?" He would take all the books and papers on the desk and toss them in the air. "You did not know nothing, you did not know what you were doing Mr. Substitute. Fuck you" and he would walk out of the room.

It was 9.15 in the morning. Jovani came in running. He had gone round the room three times before the whole class came in.

"Jovani, why did I have to tell you many times each lesson to sit down? You better sit down now or else you were out of here, and you would be sitting out side the principal's office." He ran round, took another student's pen went to his seat.

"Mr Alpha, Jovani had taken my pen" complained Heidi.

"Go give the pen back. You were a really bully. You did not jug items from people's hand by force. If you needed some one's property, you asked the person for permission to use it" Alpha said calmly.

"I did not take it by force" Jovani would reply"

"Yes, you did" she said forcefully. Jovani got up walked up to her and pulled her hair up. "You did not talk while I was talking to Mr. Alpha." Alpha went up to him and pulled him away. "That was your last chance, you sit down now, or I called the principal to take you out of here. You gave the pen back before you went to your seat.

"But I needed it, I had no pen to write with" he complained.

"I would give you a pencil to write with." Alpha assured him.

"I did not want to write with a pencil" he protested.

"You could have that pen" Heidi told him.

"I was going to sit down now and did my work" he said as he walked to his seat.

"You better did that, so that you could improve your grade.

"We did not do any work in the Basement in Ms Theorado's room.

Theoni with her pot belly, who looked like pregnant in the 7th grade, she played up all the time. She had a short attention span and she wanted to be seen and noticed by the teacher and so she would not sit in her seat. She would sit on the desk, lie on her desk if given the chance, stood by the window, or fiddling with something.

Mr. Alpha had some sympathy for her, with the thought that she was pregnant at such an early age. She liked to walk around the room. She never showed interest in any thing, nor wanted to do any class work at all. Everything seemed boring to her. "This class was boring" she would complain.

"Theoni, if you did not do work, you would not get a pass grade" Alpha would say to her.

"I did not do anything in the first quarter, but I got a "B" grade. "Those grades were given by the resource teacher Ms Theorado in the basement. "We never did no class work in her room. We did what we wanted to do. She gave us grades for being good in class. Jovani was always playing around, that was why he got a bad grade. I would start doing your work tomorrow so that I would improve my grade in your class." she would promise and then returned to her seat.

It was 11.55 in the morning Alpha went to open the door for the fourth period to come in. In came Andy and Vicena. Andy went straight to the window, opened it, and then looked at Alpha who was looking straight at him. He raised both hand up into the air. "I was not throwing anything out. I would be good today. Give me the class work, I would sit down and did all of it" he would promise. He walked back to his seat. All the students came in the usual rowdy manner from the Gym. Open the windows it's hot in here, complained the big and noisy guys.

Alpha returned to the door, to look out for those who drifted late into class and to lock the door from intruders. He looked along the corridor. Moisquito and Andrew were wrestling in the Hall way he screamed at them. They came into class and sat on the desks of empty seats for absent students. "Go to your seat" he shouted. They went to their seats reluctantly. Moisquito sat with his very long legs on the desk.

Alpha came to him and told him to put down his feet. "Dam, you told me to seat down and now you came back to me again. Why were you picking on me? he got up went to the next row, near the window sat down again forcefully. He pushed the desk forcefully, tipping Shear's book bag over. She nearly fell over herself. She got up and screamed at Moisquito, then pushed his desk back angrily, took her bag from the floor. Moisquito got up to stop her; the whole class got rowdy cheering up the fight.

Alpha went over and stood between them and then screamed at every one to go back to their seats and be quiet. By the time he got to his desk, every one was back in their seats and quiet down. The bell rang for the beginning of the "B" lunch. It was not time to match them to the cafeteria, but Shear got up and left the room, she was followed by all the girls. "You would all get cut slips" Alpha warned the girls, who left without saying a word.

Omar screamed aloud, Alpha went up to him "Why were you screaming in class?"

He looked at Alpha with empty looks "I didn't know," he replied with vagueness.

"Did you realize that your behavior was out of the way and not acceptable in class?" You should not and could not talk on top of your voice. I have told you before that there was no deaf person in here. You could talk with a normal voice, and I would hear and everyone else would hear you"

"That was how I talked. I could not do nothing about it, he ran out of the room screaming down the corridor.

CHAPTER SEVEN

It was the first week in March when Alpha was again sent to this large and populous High School, in the same classroom with the same students. He reported early at the reception desk. He was told to do late comers duty instead of professional team meeting which he knew was still going on at the same time in the morning. He wanted to protest but he decided to keep quiet. He went upstairs and received a hearty welcome from Mr. Bean again the next door teacher. He received a big hand shake and a hug. The two white colleagues in the team looked on with cold eyes.

The inclusion white teacher came into the homeroom and she showed disappointing gestures and body language. "Oh my god" she exclaimed in a disappointing voice. She put her right hand over her face, like making silent prayers. She walked to the student, talked to him and walked out without saying a word to Alpha or taking notice of his presence. The Cock and head of the team came over and brought some flyers gave them to Alpha to give to the students. He did not welcome Alpha, he was more official and business like. But his voice and countenance gave him up.

Alpha went down stairs. The assistant Principal of the ninth Grade saw him and gave him a cold shoulder.

The principal came by, he walked past, he said hi to the teacher next to Alpha, and walked away without taking notice of Alpha's presence. The Guidance counselor came by, welcomed Alpha back, and told him that it was the same assignment he had before. Alpha was still waiting for late comers, when the secretary came round and told him that the assignment was only for the day. And that he would be called out next morning for another assignment.

Alpha went to Mr. Bean to explain to him what he had been told and what he was told in the morning before the left his house. Mr. Bean directed him to the Union building representative. Alpha went round looking for him.

The Head of department came in to welcome Alpha and told him that the teacher had left and that she was not coming back. He talked to Alpha heartily, made him feel welcomed back. But Alpha did not tell Mr Fuso what he had been told. He assured Alpha that it was a vacancy he was filling in.

Alpha told him that it was not a vacancy the secretary said.

"You were here to stay" Mr. Fuso told him. He showed him the stationary the lady teacher left in a hurry. She was not coming back. I was not sure what was going on, but I knew that it was a vacancy. I knew that for sure, because the teacher talked to me before she left. I was not sure what was going on downstairs but any way I would get you some stationary to carry on" he walked out.

Next morning, Alpha did not wait for the call, he called himself. He was told that it was indeed a vacancy, but that the principal said he did not want Alpha in that position. "Why didn't you talk to the Principal himself about the vacancy?" Alpha promised to complain, because they were discriminating against him, he thought.

He was angry, but he needed the money." I had been with the district for nearly five years now, they still treated me as a new comer.

Alpha was in his room, two students were on the computer. The bell rang for the end of the lunch break.

He went out to get the students into the room.

"Get into your classrooms" shouted the assistant Principal Mr. Dwartie, who stood in the middle of the corridor. As the students went, Alpha followed leaving the door open. Mr. Hoof came over and stood by the assistant Principal and asked him "was he coming back into this room?" tilting his head towards Alpha, Mr. Dwartie shook his head, and walked away. "I knew it, I knew it" Mr. Hoof shouted as he walked towards Ms Odoojie's room. "Thank God, I was not sure, and I did not believe what I was told. Oh Ho" he said in a loud voice, and then walked into Ms Odoojie's room with fast and jubilant steps. Alpha could hear a big laughter and voices of contentment.

The next day Alpha was sent to the Tupperware Center. The classes were very large the first class he had had 32 students. There were not enough seats. The size of the class and the number of students in the class made it difficult for Alpha to keep control, and manage behavior problems effectively. Since there were not enough seats, some students used it as an excuse to disrupt the class. Some students came up to Alpha to pretend to ask questions, or asked for help, but to distract him and slow the progress of the lesson. They also did that to distract him from those throwing paper balls around the room.

The first lesson was complete disaster. He did not know the names of the students; some gave him false names as was always the case with a substitute teacher. He hardly kept control, and could do very little because some students had to sit on the windows and some on the desks of their friends. "How could you possibly teach in a crowded class room with more than ten students without seats" he thought. The day ended as it begun, each group was not only very large, but full of disruptive students, some of whom had to share seats with friends.

Alpha talked with loud voice, but there was so much noise that those at the back could hardly hear him.

Each day Alpha wrote two to three referrals of students with extreme behavior that never had any effect on the general behavior of these students. Some were too lazy, immature and others were years below grade level performance, some worked at night and came to school in the morning quite sleepy and tired. "I only came to school because I had to and I did not want my mom scolded for not coming to school," one student told Alpha.

One of the students came up to the desk stood before Alpha "Mr. Alpha why did you keep writing me up?" asked Ojay, I had no chair to sit on, and you knew that right. And you were not doing anything about it. I could not do my class work, because I have no desk to write on. Darren did not want to do any work and he would not let me use the desk to do my class work. Those boys in the corner were making all the noise, and you were blaming me for everything. It's not fair I was going home to tell my mom.

"Sir, why didn't you get more chairs and desks into this room or get rid of some students, especially those who were playing up? Heidi told Alpha in a soft voice.

Soon Alpha had had six students round his desk. "Go back to your seats" he said in a loud voice. I could only deal with one student at a time. "I needed a chair" shouted Heather.

"I would get you a chair" Alpha assured her. "No I needed it now. Call the principal to come and see what was going on now. You should not let this go on any longer.

Alpha moved away from his desk. He stood in front of the class."I have asked for more desks and chairs for this room. I have been told to wait until the registration period was over." Alpha was still talking when the door opened. In came Mr. Fuso the head of department and he looked round the room, two students sat on the window. He was not pleased with what he saw, "how was everything in here?" he asked Alpha looking into Alpha's eyes for a reaction.

"Well, sort of" replied Alpha. "Except that I needed more chairs and desks for some of my students who had no seats."

"How many students do you have in each group?" he asked again looking at Alpha.

"I had an average of 29. I had 32 in group one, 31 in group three, and 29 in this group and there were only 24 seats in the room."

Mr. Fuso counted the number of students in the room and the number of desks needed for every student in the room.

"Have you complained that you had too many students in this room?" he asked in a commanding voice. The room was not big enough for the number of students in it and students should not have to sit two to a chair and on the windows. Had anyone came in here to look at this situation as it was? This was not acceptable by any standards, I would not let that happened in here.

"I have asked for more chairs and desks. I told Mr. Dwartie the assistant principal that I have 32 students in class and there were only 24 seats." Mr. Fuso cleared his throat he had another look round the room. He counted the number of students the second time. "This was a very large class indeed" he said in a low voice.

"Alright, I would come back tomorrow to sort that out. But remember, our contract said we could not have more than 29 students in a class. Even that was too large to control under normal circumstances. I would see you tomorrow first period." He turned round to go, stopped and looked at Alpha "remember if any student disrupted you class write them up."

The last period was all chaos. The students were restless, besides the fact that they did not have enough seats. Two students who had been sharing the same chair started a fight, which Alpha went to stop. There was commotion in the class, Alpha called for help, but no one came being near the end of the school day. Four students standing at the back of the room started gambling with quarters. Alpha went there to stop them. "Sir, we had no seats to do our work" One of them complained. Tiffany had her walkman very loud; Alpha went to her to take it away.

"You give that to me" he said in a commanding voice and stretching out his right hand.

"No sir, look at those boys, they were making all the noise, you were not doing anything about it. You should send them out of the room." she said.

"I could not send them out because if they got involved in any mischief, I would be responsible" he told her. "But some other teachers threw out the trouble makers" she insisted. She took the walkman off her head, held it in her hand and walked to her seat.

Alpha screamed to get the students to be quiet without success. He went round to get the students to sit down. "How could we sit down when there were no seats" one boy complained.

Alpha screamed again to get every one to be quiet. The noise went even higher. He called the office the second time for help, but no one came. He gave up and went to his seat. He sat down writing some referrals. He was soon surrounded by eight students whose intentions were to confuse him with different requests so that some students at the back of the room could do some mischief without him noticing who did what. Some students wanted to know who he was writing up and possibly to steal the referral forms from his desk.

An administrator came in, he was upset the class was too noisy. Students were not in their seats.

"There were not enough seats in the class for all the students to seat down" Alpha told him.

"That was beside the point," he said angrily. "Could I talk to you outside the room." They went outside the room. "Mr. Alpha, you were not keeping control of you class. This was not acceptable" he said angrily.

Alpha's voice was now faint from repeated shouting to keep the class under control.

"If you could not keep control of the class, how could you teach?" Mr. Wang said in an angry voice.

Alpha tried to explain to him that the class was too large, and not enough seats, some students were standing at the back of the room. He did not listen and accept that that was the source of the problem but he told Alpha that he was not doing his job effectively and that he was expecting much more from him and he should control the class.

Alpha knew that he could not control so large a class with so many demotivated students, some of them had no seats and they were using that as an excuse to disrupt the lesson. Some of the students were marking time to avoid been sleepy and dosing off in class. Alpha did not know the names of the students in the class and some of them gave him wrong names so that he could not write them up.

The assistant principal was not interested in the seating problem, but the fact that Alpha had called twice from the same room in the same period meant that he was not in control of the class.

He came back into the classroom, looked round the room and probably did not notice or turned a blind eye to those students who were sharing seats and those sitting on the windows who had no seats.

"Write up those that disrupted your lesson and send the referrals to me he walked away. Alpha returned to his desk the referrals file had gone. The bell rang and all the students ran out of the room. Alpha found the empty file behind the heater.

He rearranged the seats and left. He walked down the stairs without noticing any one, nor saw any of the administrators. He had complete burn out and when he got into his car, he felt so low that he thought he had lost a whole months energy in one day. He felt that he was totally burned out and a feeling of lifelessness seemed to overwhelm him.

It was the end of a usual bad school day which he experienced nearly every school day as things never got better as a substitute teacher. The going was getting harder and harder each day. It was evident that his effort and dedication were not appreciated by anybody from the officers in the main district office through the rank and file in the school and right down to the students in class, all did not think much of him as a substitute teacher, especially a black man with an accent.

CHAPTER EIGHT

The Wednesday morning started bright and sunny, Alpha left his home at the usual time. He got to school parked his car and went up stairs to sign on, picked his homeroom folder and turned round to walk to his classroom.

"Good morning" said Ms Peterson with a false smile. Alpha turned round and he replied with the same smile.

"Were you here permanently?" she asked

"I was not too sure" he replied. "I had the five years state professional teachers' certificate" he told her. "Well, this should be it I think it was a vacancy you were filling in. Let's hope you got this job" she said. Alpha had mixed feelings. My classes were too large and very difficult to handle he told himself. He walked on to his room he forgot to put the referrals he wrote at home for four students. He opened the door to let in the students and walked back quickly into the office, placed the referrals and returned to his room. He overheard the assistant principal telling one of the teachers next door that Alpha's students made too much noise and he wrote too many referrals. "Hmm, but some of these students were a real pain in the butt I knew that for sure" the man replied.

Alpha was standing where he could not be seen. He thought of going in to defend himself, but changed his mind. He moved on, as one student approached. He walked into his room. The bell rang for the start of the first period.

The class was packed full as before, Alpha waited until all the students sat down. "I have no seat complained one of the students. "I was sitting on the window" shouted Albertito and Alpha had no solution.

One student took out play cards and spread them on the desk. "Did not start Jesus" it's too early for that. "I would take them away and you might not get them back. You better put them in your book bag, come give out the dittos for me" Alpha told the boy who still held the cards in his hand.

He came up took the dittos and he was walking away when Alpha said "give one to each student."

He gave half the class" I was tired, if any one wanted one, you come get it" he tossed the rest of the dittos on the desk next to Alpha and went to his seat. He danced meringue. "Go to your seat please" Alpha said to him.

It was near the end of the period when Mr. Fuso walked into the class. He found the class packed full. "Gee!" he said in a surprised voice. "Were these all in your class?" he asked.

"Yes, they were" Alpha replied.

"No way, I would not let you have these many students in one class. This was far more than any teacher could handle. How did they expect you to be effective, if you had so large a class. They were not doing any thing about it. I was going to have a grievance report form for you. That was the only way this would be corrected. The class was too large and there were not enough seats for all the students. I as head of department would not let you carry on in this condition."

The bell rang the students rushed out. Mr Fuso left as well.

In came period three Alpha stood by the door watching the students came in. He stood there until all the students had entered the room. "I was not sharing a seat today" Sassah told Alpha. "You should have enough seats for all the students in your class by now. I was going to sit on your desk Sassah said if I did not have a seat. Call the Principal to come and sort out the seating places for all the students in the class." she sat on Alpha's desk with both hands on the desk, swinging her feet.

"Come to your seat Sassah. You were holding up the lesson." One boy shouted from the back.

"Alright I was sorry sir. I knew it's not your fault, but you should let them know that there were not enough seats in your room." She walked to the back of the room and sat down.

Alpha wrote the topic on the board, and then gave out the dittos. "Albertito, keep quiet" Alpha said in a raised voice.

"Oh! You knew our names already?" he said from the back.

"Well, I knew the names of those that play up all the time in class. Alpha called the class attendance list, and by the time he completed the attendance list, the dittos were flying all over the room. The usual disruptive students had folded their dittos into paper balls and were stoning each other with them. "Juana it was not a good behavior to throw paper ball around the room.

"I would collect all the paper balls in the class Mr. Alpha; would you give me extra credit for doing that?" Sagioto asked as he got up to clean the room. He collected a hand full of the paper balls. "Albertito threw a ball at me." He threw all the paper balls in his hand one after the other at Albertito in rapid succession. Albertito got up and charged at him. Alpha rushed between them. He sent both of them out of the class to the office.

Chris came up to Alpha and asked for another ditto. "I gave you one before. Didn't I? Alpha asked in a raised voice.

"Juana took it and threw it away." He replied in an arrogant and defiant voice, as if it was not his responsibility.

"I was not giving you another ditto, sorry. You should have been reading the ditto you decided to use it as a paper ball. "I did not throw it, Juan did"

"How could you allow him to take your ditto and threw it away? You knew that if you did the class work you got credit for it."

"Sir, he did that all the time. He took it by force, and he was bigger than me. Oh well, I was not doing your work then he walked away with angry steps.

"Look here, you did this work to get credits, which you needed to go to the next class. You got that clear. If you did not do it, I would not give you credit. It's your responsibility to earn credits" Alpha said to him.

He stopped, turned round to Alpha. "Who cared?" he replied abruptly. "Fuck you" he turned round and went to his seat. "I was doing no work" he said aloud as he sat down.

Shrize came up to Alpha "May I have a ditto, Mr. Alpha."

"What happened to the one I gave you before?"

"You never gave me one. Brandon gave you one didn't he?"

"No he did not give me one" she insisted.

"Yes, I gave you one" shouted Brandon from the corner. "She was the first one to throw her ditto across.

"Listen class" Alpha said in a loud voice so that every one would hear him. "Greg, would you listen please I was talking, you had to pay attention."

"But we were talking too, why were you interrupting us?' Greg said to Mr. Alpha.

"Shut your mouth" shouted Lizada from the front row.

"This was not acceptable, not every one in here wanted to sit in a filthy room littered with paper balls. I did not like it, and I was sure there were some students in here who did not like to see all these bits of paper around them.

Andy got up. "I would pick them all up" he shouted. He went round, picked all the paper balls, and filled his pickets and both hands. He emptied his hands into the Garbage can. "Empty your pockets as well" Alpha told him. "No sir, they were safe in here. No one would reach them. I would not throw them around. I promised" He went back to his seat with those paper balls in his pockets.

. Andy could you empty your pockets and put the paper balls in the garbage Alpha told him.

"No body would reach them where they were." He assured Alpha.

Jesus took a paper from under his desk and threw it at Andy, which hit him on the left eye.

Andy took the paper balls from his pocket and hit Jesus one after another in rapid succession until he emptied his pockets. Alpha threw Jesus and Andy out of the room again.

Reggieda got up, came to Mr. Alpha "could I go out as well?" Alpha looked at him with disgusting eyes. "Go back to your seat" he commanded in a raised voice.

"Did not scream at me, you had no right to scream at me what did you think you were? You were just a Substitute teacher." He walked out of the room. Greg got up, "I was going out as well and he ran out of the door.

The class settled down a little. Alpha introduced the lesson, and went through the ditto. He kept an eye on the boys at the back of the room. They were up to something he told himself. He went and stood by them.

"Go back to your desk" shouted Rodney we did not want you back here.

"Write the answers on the board Mr. Alpha, and we will copy them on the ditto" said Johnny. "Leave those who were fooling around alone and concentrated on us who wanted to learn.

"Thank you Johnny. That was what I wanted to hear. I did know that some students made a deliberate effort to stop the lesson."

"It was not just in your class, they did that all the time, and in every class all day and every day" added Johnny.

"They confused the teacher, so that you did not teach, and they got away with it in every class. They did not get written up. I was not happy with that I came to school to learn and not to fool around."

"My mom would beat me up if I fooled around, she told me. My mom wanted me to graduate and went on to college" added Stephanie.

"Shut up your mouth" shouted Carla from the back seat. "You were talking trash. Were you trying to get extra credit from the teacher? if you didn't then shut your mouth. I would box your face after school today for being stupid in class said Andre. You were talking garbage"

"Why did you not come and box me now" she replied angrily. "I was not afraid of you. I knew you were a bully, but I could stand up to you. If you did hit me, I would get my brother to beat you up on the street. He would come and waited for you outside the school he was bigger and stronger than you."

Andre got up, "Beat me on the street? You must be kidding. Tell him to come. He would be carried home in a bag. My group members would blow his head out in minutes."

Alpha got up and walked to Carla. "Stop that nonsense talks and keep quiet. You should concentrate on what you were doing." Alpha told her. "You better tell him to stop provoking me."

"Send them out" shouted a voice from the back. "We were not interested in what they were saying.

Alpha went round helping some students to complete the ditto. "Could you write the answers on the board so that we could copy them on the ditto." asked Brandon.

"If I wrote all the answers on the board and you copied them in your ditto, what would you have done?" Alpha told the class.

"But that was what other teachers did. They made it easy for us."

"I would then give you credit for just coping the answers from the board."

"We got credit for doing nothing in other classes, as long as you behaved yourself. That was how it went you got a "C" grade as the least for behaving in class. Mr. Hurton gave me a "B" for behaving well in his class. I had never done any class work or home work for him" Alejandro said proudly.

Alpha went to the board to write the answers for some of the questions on the ditto. I would not give you the answers to all the questions, no way he told the class. You needed to earn a credit by doing some individual work in class.

Some students sat quietly copying, while others did not even copy the answers. At the end of the period, he took some dittos neatly filled up, while others were half way filled up, some with two lines filled up, some with only the names written on the ditto, other had nothing written on them. He used these clean and unwritten dittos for the next class.

It was the last period of the day, the group came in noisily. Two Hispanic students came in dancing to Hispanic music. They danced before the class. Alpha stopped them and told them to go to their seats.

"This was the last period I am tired. I did not want to do any more work for today" said Anna as she walked to her middle row seat. She sat on the desk. Alpha told her to sit down. She then sat with her feet on the desk. "That was not how you sat in class" Alpha told her. "Put your feet down."

"No this was how I wanted to sit down" she protested

"Well, you had a choice, either you put your feet down and sit properly or go outside." he said in a commanding voice.

Anna sucked her teeth, then put her feet down and turned her back toward the blackboard.

"You were holding up the class, Anna. Do what you were told to do and sit properly like the rest of us" Tisha told Anna.

"What the hell was this?" she exploded. "You told me to sit down I did. You told me to put my feet down I did. What the hell you were picking on me? I hated you, I hated your class black substitute" she said in a shouting voice.   She got up angrily, took her bag, pushed the desk angrily, and walked out of the class with angry steps.

The lesson went on. Marcosa was beating the desk at interval in the back. Alpha looked at him with reproaching eyes he smiled. "I was sorry" he said raising his hands into the air in a surrender manner.

The class ended as it started, with very little cooperation from the students.

Alpha breathed a sigh of relief at the end of the day. He cleaned the board, and he was rearranging the desks when Mr Fuso came back in. He pulled out the Grievance form neatly filled in. He asked Alpha to sign it.

Alpha had some inner doubts about the effects of the grievance form on his position in the school. I could be made a scape goat for this he thought. He sat down, signed the form, and Mr. Fuso left. He filled in the referral forms, which he took to the office, dropped them. He then left for home with a doubtful mind as to the effects of the grievance report.

Next morning, Alpha had a surprised call from Human resources. "I was sending you to Bhutto High School

Alpha was not sure why they changed his position so soon, without an explanation. He thought something must have happened. He guessed that the grievance form had not been taken in good spirit. "I knew I was a victim of circumstances. "Why was I going to Bhutto school" he asked.

"It was a directive. I still had a long list of Substitutes to post out. Have a good day" the phone went dead.

Alpha had mixed feelings about his new assignment. He had been to this school before, but the manner and timing were a bit disturbing. I did not initiate the grievance report to be victimized for it. It was true that the classes were too large to manage.

This was what the system was all about. You did the dirty work. No body recognized what you did, from the Principal the Lord of the manor down to colleagues. You should never complain or say any negative statement about any thing especially if you were a substitute teacher. You should not write referrals no matter what happened in your classes, you got victimized.

As a substitute teacher you had no voice, no say on just about anything you should not call for help, the students could say anything to you and behaved in any way in your class because you were not a teacher and had no rights. You as a substitute teacher were at the mercy of the school administration and you could be replaced at any time with just a simple phone call. The fact that Alpha was a black African man with an accent made him extremely vulnerable in an overt racist environment.

No one wanted to talk to him from the students to the school administrators because of his accent which was like an open smelly wound which no one wanted to witness or be close to. The substitute teacher was to be invisible and not heard of by the school lords and he should endour any problems that he encountered along the way and not complained to keep his position in the school.

Mr. Alpha got up from his bed and the thought of his job made him felt sick. Why was I different from the rest of the substitutes, I have all the qualifications and experience for the job but they still treated me with snobbish attitudes.

The fact was that black African substitutes like Alpha were considered as outsiders. White substitutes could complain and did speak their minds to the school administrators without any serious consequences and they would be listened to and any complaints investigated and sorted out.

Alpha felt some hot blood ran down his spine as he tried to figure out what was really going on with his career.

He was confused temporarily, and then he felt better within himself. He looked at the clock. He dressed up quickly, took his bag and went down stairs and out to the car. He accepted his fate as a substitute teacher and a Blackman with an accent who could not change anything and could not do anything about his situation.

"Oh God help me please" he said aloud. He turned the engine on, backed off the car into the street. "Oh God be with me and forgive me" he thought over what was going on in that class room. It was real hell over there. "I was not going to get anywhere with those students. The situation was not going to get better; rather it would have got worst. God help me" he said aloud before he went through the traffic light. "I hoped it was for a good course that I had been moved to another school yet again. Things would get better by Gods grace he said.

CHAPTER NINE

THE NEXT MORNING WHICH was Wednesday Alpha had the call to go to the school down town. He left the house in good time to get to the school. He got to the ground floor car park. He looked at his watch, 7.55 am. "I would be the first person to arrive at the school he thought. He locked the car and walked to the escalator. He went up to the third floor. He walked to the desk, the secretary asked him the name of the teacher he came in to Substitute for. She gave him the teachers list to look for the name of the teacher. He looked through, it was not there. He then repeated the name of the teacher to her Ms. Forge "Oh, it's the Colonial School." she told him. "That was where you were" pointing to the other side of the floor, with four rooms lined up. "The principal was Mr. Davidson; he would take care of you. This was another school.

Alpha went over and sat on the chair by the Principal's door he took out his newspaper and was reading it.

A boy came up to him. "Excuse me" he said Alpha lifted his head. "Who were you substituting for today?" he asked Alpha. Without answering he said "the principal would be in later on" the boy said and then he walked away.

Alpha got up and walked to the bathroom, it was full of graffiti and the toilets were run down he felt like not have a pee (wee) again because of the condition of the bathrooms and decided to keep it and held it until later in the day and he came back and sat down went on scanning his newspaper.

Another student came up to him and asked "who were you substituting for?"

Ms. Forge" Alpha replied.

"Oh Ms Forge was absent today, great" he walked away.

Alpha looked at the watch 8.20 already and no one to talk to. Mr Bee came up to Alpha, shook his hand. "You had been here before" he told Alpha. "Yes for sure" Alpha replied.

"Well, my name was Bee. Did you want me to show you the time table schedule" he asked.

"Yes please" Alpha replied and he got up and walked behind Mr. Bee into one classroom.

"You had first block free. You had second block in here and third and fourth blocks next door.

"Thank you Mr Bee." He said calmly. Mr Bee walked away; Alpha followed him out of the room. "I was free till 9.54" he told himself. I wondered where to sit until then." he asked himself. Alpha walked back to Mr Bee and asked him where to sit down, and did some work. "We had no teacher's room, but this was where we sat down and did some work." He led Alpha into a classroom, used as a store as well. He opened the door, "you can sit in here and did your work."

"Thank you Mr Bee, he said in a polite voice. Alpha walked into the room with a few chairs scattered around. The room had piles of copy paper; boxes piled high cartoons all over the room and three tables and chairs. He sat down, but the door kept opening and closing constantly, as students came in and out. It was the fourth time Alpha had been in the school, with no apparent changes in the set up. The previous three occasions, he got his class schedule on a scrap of paper in pencil. This time he had to copy it from the classroom schedule on the wall.

The school was very small, less than a hundred students he saw around the one unit. There were three classrooms, in effective use, no teachers lounge and no planner. Graffiti everywhere .the building was an old office building turned into two schools with no conversions and adjustments for classroom use.

It was in the heart of the commercial city district, no indications on the outside that it was a school building for two separate schools. There was a single bathroom for students and teachers. The bathroom walls were filled with Graffiti. The environment looked like a run down building, waiting to be demolished.

The appearance of the building and the environment around the school was a good indicator of the attitudes of its students and teachers. Alpha met students who were expelled from all the other schools, on the school recycle bin.

These were students who teachers wrote up every day for various disciplinary problems, and were doing very poorly in those schools. "Recycling these students in less commodious surroundings like these, only increased their frustrations and hopelessness."

Alpha observed that the classroom doors had no locks. The barriers between classrooms were movable stage screens that students rolled over.

Students crossed from one classroom to another at will. He observed that a lot of the students spent a good deal of time on the large corridor socializing. When in the classroom the students moved across the barriers to talk to one another, pass letters, drawings from one classroom to another. Alpha had a class in the middle room the Principal was in the next room substituting for an absent teacher. Alpha had an extra big student who talked with a very heavy voice. He was not only noisy, but rude and argumentative. Alpha had told him more than three times to lower his voice, without success.

The principal in the next room across the barrier instead of coming over to tell the student to be quiet wrote a note and gave it to one female student to deliver to the boy. She came through the barrier and handed the note to Donald. "Mr. Davidson told me to give you this."

Donald read it aloud to the class "you were too loud" the note said. "I was too loud! What the heck?"

There were not enough seats for all the students they used one of the tables to seat. One of the tables was pushed over by the students. Alpha ran to catch it, since the legs seemed not holding the table firmly he took the leg that fell over and tried to fix it. The leg was barely supporting the table.

Alpha discovered that the table in front of the class, next to the teacher's desk had one leg very short. He moved the two heavy history books on it and he discovered that the desk was falling over. He put back the books quickly in the center of the desk to stabilize it. He tried to fix it but the leg was too short he walked away from it.

Alpha was again called out to go to the same school but in the section that was nested in a commercial setting to substitute for another teacher. He left his house early next morning since he did not know where he was going. He got to school a lot too early and he went into the main building housing the two mushroom schools sharing the same facilities in the old office block. He reported for work at the receptionist desk. The Lady looked at her absent teacher list. "It was not for this school" she told Alpha. "You sit on the chair and wait for the Principal he would soon be here"

Alpha sat on the chair outside the Principal's office again. He waited, and waited. Teachers began to come in, and walked straight into their rooms, without signing. . There was no teachers' room, and no Receptionist. He waited until the Principal came in after a while. "Who were you in for?" he asked. "It was in the hotel on the other side" he told Alpha.

"I would leave my car here, and walk over there." said Alpha.

"Oh no, you could not, it was raining; besides it was a long way from here, and it's not that easy to find." He explained to Alpha how to get there. "I would see you over there later" he went into his office.

Alpha looked at his watch, and then went into the escalator.

He parked the car in the parking lot in a hurry and walked round without remembering the exact location where he parked his car.

He got lost and he went back into the hotel desk; he went up and down the escalators. He looked at his watch, it was already 8.40. "I was late already" he told himself. He saw two security officers going up the escalators and he decided to ask them. He followed them, but by the time he got up to them, they had disappeared. He looked for another security guard. He saw one walking fast he was walking up to him when he came upon another one. He asked him for the directions to the school in the hotel. "It's at the basement of the hotel, by the railway track. You had to go outside and walk down the stairs to get to it.

Alpha walked into the school finally after several attempts. The school had three class rooms, no windows and only one door for exit and entrance. He signed up this time and walked into the teachers lounge sweating. He looked round for source of fresh air but there were no windows.

There were two small tables "Hmm," he exclaimed "a school without windows and only one exit door."

The classrooms had only one door way. The classrooms were trapezium shaped with office wheeled chairs and trapezium shaped desks for students.

Coming outside of the school, you came face to face with the water way and the zoo pond a few fee below the tracks and the embankment.

The staff were friendly they offered him coffee for the first time in five years. It was a real surprise, unlike in most other schools where the Substitutes were seen as nonentities, not real teachers and were considered as outsiders the assistant principal came and chatted with Alpha, which he found quite unusual and strange. He had never had a word with a principal or administrator in all the schools he had substituted in. She made him felt welcomed and wanted. "I felt, I was a real teacher for the first time" he told himself.

The day went well he spent an hour in the Kiosk with two female students who went out there by turn to socialize and introduce basic items and T-shirts to the public and hoteliers.

Alpha left the school in the afternoon to get his car. He went into the car park and could not find the location where he left his car. He went to the park attendants' office. "I could not find my car" he told the lady. "What happened to it?" she asked. "I parked it in a hurry this morning, and did not remember where I parked it.

He was given a security guard to go with him in a truck to locate his car. They drove round until they found where he parked it.

CHAPTER TEN

THE IDEA OF BEING on the road each day for years was getting on Alpha and he was wondering what he was going to do about it. Those who came after him had long got permanent jobs and he was still a daily substitute.

He was wondering constantly what to do next when the idea came to him that he had been told by another officer in the school department at the time of his hiring that he would never get help from school administrators. But it was worst in this particular school, because these two men would make his life a living hell so that he would be ineffective and then they would turn round and blamed him for not doing his job as expected of him.

And in the end they would justify his ineffectiveness because he was black and black teachers were never as effective as white teachers and so they were doing everything to prove their point.

It was a label black people carried around in every situation and work place in this environment. Being black was a thorn in every white person's butt to have to deal with you when they did not think much about you and they doubted very much your intelligence, output and effectiveness

The school administrators would do every thing possible to prove that black teachers were inferior and not as effective as white teachers since students too discriminated against black teachers. Each time you a black teacher came to class the students would make negative remarks, "what was this black man doing here, were you a teacher, I did not want a black teacher, Why did they send us a black man, I hated black teachers, Where was our teacher" were some of the remarks you heard from students especially black students who had more negative attitudes towards Alpha in every school he went into.

To the people who mattered in this environment, your qualifications and experience did not come into the equation and those qualities had nothing to do with their own assessment of you from the color syndrome background which they used to put all black people especially those with an accent in the basket of idiots and non English speakers according to American standards.

It was late Saturday afternoon, when Alpha met with Mrs. Garbla who was next door to his room in the third floor. All what she said to him the very first day he came into the school had come to pass. Alpha felt relieved when he discovered that there were complaint after complaint about those two assistant principals. Alpha was sent back to Abedone school for the second time without explanations as usual.

"I knew you were not going to last long in that room. I knew what was coming for you there had been complaints after complaints, about those two men in that building. Even their fellow white colleagues whispered complaints about their inconsistent behavior in dealing with teachers' complaints. They would willingly attend to complaints from those teachers they had high regard for and would listened to them and talked to them but for you the back sheep, they always pretended to be busy so that they would not talk to you and attended to your concerns.

Their daily work was all around the color syndrome phobia which filled their blood, attitudes and work habits.

I told you before that those men would make your life a hell hole. That was what they did to every black teacher that came into this school. But guess what, they employed a white teacher as usual, but she rarely came to school. I had not seen her more than twice a week. It's the same old story of having substitutes all the time for that room.

It was three years now, they had not got a permanent teacher in that room. You stayed longer than any other teacher in that room for the past three years.

The vacancy existed but they did not want to fill it with some one whom the two big boys did not like. They preferred substitutes all the time and manipulated the situation and kept control of the selection.

The interest of the students was not important. Each teacher had a different teaching method and approach to the subject matter. It was strange that the District would allow this to go on at the expense of the students.

They were aware that the students were the losers. The students came and went without learning anything. They knew that, but they had to maintain this rotation of teaching methods and ideas to keep the lid on.

Most of the students went to high school with no basic educational foundation. But of course, the subject matter was not all that important in the system as I knew it; the emphasis was who was who in the system, and personality identification.

The importance of each administrator in the school was the only thing that stood out most prominent in this school system.

You as a black man with an accent stood no chance in the District and nobody wanted to know about your existence."

"I have had these experiences now and again" said Alpha. "It was something I found very disturbing. The students felt that you did not know anything, because you had an accent. They sometimes asked you if you could speak English. A student had told Alpha that we did not want that Liberian accent in here, please speak proper English so that we could understand you. Alpha took his time to explain as he had done before.

I spent many years in Europe. I spoke the English of the British people. I did not speak like an American with the American accent because I was not one of them. I was trying to retain my identity. But I did not think that I was not speaking the English you spoke, but you could not read or write what you spoke.

It was lunch time in the school and the students were coming from the gym, and they were still full of active energy. They came in disorderly, and were not ready for any class work. Alpha had shouted repeatedly to get the class to settle down but all in vain. He banged the table repeatedly in vain to get their attention. He had enough, he took the phone and call for an administrator. He had a few students sat down. No one came, the noise went on and he could not introduce the lesson.

It was time to take the students down for the B lunch. He came back, opened and door, closed it behind him and he was walking to his desk when the door opened.

In came Mr. Brauno, the assistant Principal, breathing heavily like a fattened pig on a hot summer afternoon. He was almost out of breath when he came close to Alpha. You could see the signs of anger on his face.

"You were the worst teacher I had ever known. You could not keep control of your students. You wrote too many discipline referrals. Did you think we had nothing to do? You were employed and paid to teach and control the students. You were doing none of that. What did you think they brought you here for?" He was talking amid heavy breaths. He looked at Alpha eye ball to eye ball, sucked his teeth, then turned round and walked out, banging the door behind him.

Alpha stood there spelled bound for a while. He was taken off guard. He expected support from the administrators, but he got a mouthful wash instead. The unexpected antagonism from the assistant principal, who he should rely on for help baffled him and left him speechless. Alpha could not have answered back, because the school system was such that these people were like little gods, expecting teachers to worship them, especially if you were not grounded in the system he was like an extra finger in the hand, just a substitute for that matter. A substitute did not matter in the system, because there were lots of them to go round, the hidden agenda in the district.

Substitutes were sent to troubled classrooms nearly all the time. The reason was that teachers with the worst students stayed out of school many more times than teachers with cooperative and motivated students. When the teacher had well motivated and ready to learn students he would not like to take days off from school. This was because the students would miss him and he would miss the students and he would not like to break the bonds with his students. But teachers with students of varying abilities and behavior problems would always be sick and preferred to stay home many times over to recuperate.

He was used as a scape goat on every rump of the school ladder. Alpha was a substitute teacher; no one in the system treated a substitute with respect, because the word substitute carried a negative connotation of illiterate, in experience unqualified and not a real teacher.

Substitutes were seen as the people who polluted the classrooms and were responsible for poor output. But no one ever looked at their own contributions to the poor quality of the organization of the system that resulted in the poor results and the mountain of problems in every corner of the system. Every one preferred to blame someone else for the inherent problems that those who mattered turned blind eye to and impeached the blame on those below them in the chin of command and the substitute where the blame buck stopped.

It was not just the students who have no respect for Substitutes, but every rank and file in the system from top to bottom.

Alpha was very disturbed by the behavior of the assistant principal towards him. He walked to the next door teacher who was a Cape verdian and also having his lunch.

"How were you sir?" the man said to Alpha. "You looked disturbed, were the students driving you crazy?" he asked Alpha.

"No, not really"" he replied.

"Grab a chair and sit down." he said softly. Alpha took a chair and sat down, he explained carefully what had happened with Mr. Brauno.

Mr. Tee cleared his throat. "Look here, believe or not, both assistant principals were anti black," he confided in Alpha.

"Mrs. Garbla told me that, and I had seen evidence of that today.

"Oh gush; you have not seen nothing yet. That was just the beginning of what to expect. They would do anything to tell you that you were not welcomed here, as long as they were here. Mr. Brauno was the assistant principal at Irman High School, where the whole faculty matched to the to the Superintendent's office to deliver a protest letter, saying that he was too authoritative, too inquisitive and domineering.

The next day he was moved to this school. They would do anything to make your life a hell in this school. I experienced that when I first came here. I had to complain to the union twice. Someone told me to tell him off, which I did he had since left me alone.

The day ended as it started with no inroads as far as discipline was concerned. Alpha went home that afternoon with a heavy heart.

The next day Alpha met with Mr. Humbla the other assistant principal out side his classroom. "How was it going?" Mr. Humbla asked Alpha.

"I was still trying to get the students to cooperate" he replied in a relaxed voice.

"All right" he replied, "but what did you do in your spear time? Were you doing some English studies?

"No not at all" Alpha replied with a surprised voice. "I did all my studies in Europe. I had two masters' degrees from English Universities. My hobby was writing. I was writing a novel" Alpha said proudly.

"A novel" he repeated in a deep disappointing voice, he frown his face with looks of disapproval and hurried away.

This was exactly what people here believed in Alpha said to himself that an accent was equal to deficiency in English language, he thought.

"I did not really needed extra English. I lived in Europe for twelve years. English was the first language in my home country. I spoke only English" Alpha said in a soft voice.

Mr. Humbla became a regular visitor in Alpha's classroom. He visited the classroom nearly every day at first to check on seating plans, his handouts, his mark book, the lesson plans, student work, grades, homework and even work on the board he would scrutinized.

Each day he came to the class, he would check on every little thing. If he was passing by, and saw a student outside Alpha's room, he would come in and find out why the student was outside. If Alpha sent a student to the office as most teachers did to get the most disruptive students from the class, he would send the student back immediately. "Why have you come back?" Alpha would ask the student.

"Mr. Humbla told me to come back" the student would say. "Were you doing detention this afternoon for him for sending you to the office?"

Alpha would ask. "No" replied Gary. "Mr. Humbla did not tell me to stay for detention this afternoon."

Next morning Alpha came to school determined to take control of his classes, but got more frustration with the same students and the same behavior. Alpha told Gary to sit down and behaved himself. "You were not the only student in here. Why did I have to keep telling you to sit down in your seat and behaved yourself. You kept your mouth shut and stay in your seat for the rest of the period."

"Did not scream at me you had no authority to do that I would tell my mom and tell the Principal about you that you were screaming at me in your class. I bet my mom would tell the principal to fire you" the boy said aloud.

"I loved to meet your mom, and explained to her how you behaved in my class. I would tell her to come and watched how you behave in my class one of these days" Alpha told Gary.

"She would not believe you. She believed what I told her and not what you said to her. I already told her that anything that happened in the class, they always say I did it. Other students talked, swore, and walked about, but they never got written up. Teachers kept writing me up all the time. My mom did not believe that I was a bad student. I did work at home, sat down and watched TV. I went out to play when she told me to go. She would not believe what you told her about me, she would believe what I told her about you. So did not waste your time talking to her about me she would not listen to you."

"You go and sit down and keep your mouth shut. I did not want to hear a word from you again" Alpha told Gary in a commanding voice.

Gary went to his seat, he sat down took out his hand held play station.

Alpha was hoping that things would get better as time went by. Some one kicked the door twice. Alpha went to open it. Jesus stood by the door with the late slip. Alpha looked at his watch it was eleven zero five in the morning. "You were coming to class very late Jesus here we were at eleven o'clock in the morning when you should have been here at eight in the morning. You came that late to class, and you were kicking the door so that every one would notice your arrival. Did you have an excuse for coming late to class every day.

"No" he replied sharply. "Stupid" he said.

"Who was stupid" Alpha asked He gave Alpha his late pass, with no excuse circled and no detention mentioned at the bottom of the slip, Alpha signed it and gave it back to him.

Jesus was one student who liked to hug every girl he met on the corridors and in the classroom. He never brought anything to class. The book bag he hung behind his back was empty all the time. He was the first student always to fold his handout into a paper plane and threw it away round the room. He would throw any book he laid his hands on out of the window. He walked to his seat, kicked his desk. He got up walked to the girl who sat in front of him, hugged her and started playing with her hair. "Jesus, why did I have to tell you to sit down all the time? You behaved the same way each day in my classroom.

"But Mr. Alpha, I loved doing that I loved playing with girl's hair, hugging them and kissing them. That made me feel good I could not help it, and I had nothing to do about it" he went back to his seat.

"Sir, we had reported him many times to the principal about it" said Mary.

"He had been suspended for that, but he would not stop. If we pushed him away, he would come back and start a fight, for not letting him play with your hair." added Liz

Alpha sent him out of the room Jesus walked out reluctantly, pushing book bags and desks on his way out.

Alpha closed the door behind him but the student kicked the door from outside with a loud noise. Alpha opened the door again quickly "What did you think you were doing?" he asked the boy as he swung the door and held it on the inside.

"I wanted you to suspend me, I wanted to go back home now and plaid on my computer." he told Alpha.

Alpha talked to him for a while and brought him into the class. He went to his seat; he then turned round and came back to Mr. Alpha.

"I wanted you to send me home right now, suspend me please" he told Alpha. He then scattered all the piles of papers and books on Alpha's desk Alpha sent him down to the office.

Jesus went down to the office. A few minutes later he came back up and knocked at the door. Alpha went to open it "Were you going home?" Alpha asked him "No, I have been sent back to class" he said in a low voice.

He went to his seat without Alpha telling him to but he walked reluctantly and sat down angrily. He breathed heavily, looked up the ceiling, and he looked out of the window and then he hit the desk three times. Alpha came and stood by him, looked at him but he turned away. "You go away, I did not want to see you. Go to your desk" Jesus said angrily.

"But you were disturbing the class" Alpha told him.

"I was not" he replied angrily. "You were attracting attention then."

"Leave me alone. I told you to go back to your desk. I hated you. I did not want to see you. You picked on me all the time. You did not like me. I did not like you either" He pushed the desk over, making loud noise.

"You could not come to class with an attitude" Alpha told him.

"Sir, kick him out of the class. He was like that all day.

"Oh you F. off it's none of your business" he replied angrily.

"It's my business. You were disrupting the class and we could not get on.

Mr Alpha could not explain the lesson to us. The class would be quiet if Mr Alpha sent you out of the room."

"I told you to shut up." he got up walked angrily to Aaron, opened his arms in a fighting posture.

Aaron got up. "You wanted to fight?" he too opened his arms.

"Sit down Aaron" Alpha shouted to him. Aaron sat down.

"If you wanted to fight, let us go out side" Aaron told Jesus. "You meet me downstairs after school" Aaron told him.

"No let us get it on now. If you were a man enough follow me outside." He left the room and he did not return.

Katie was the last student to come to class very late each day. She came in dancing. She was a big girl about seventeen years old among eleven year olds. She was mature compared to the rest of the class. She did no class work, except looking around, joining in every conversation and talking non stop. She got upset if you told her to be quiet. "Why were you picking on me all the time? I was not disturbing any one; I was not disrupting your class. I was talking to my friends. I did not understand why I could not talk to my friends if I wanted to. Every body was picking on me all the time. Nobody seemed to like me in this school." she said angrily.

"Katie, you could take a break now you were still talking. You could let your friends did the class work" Alpha told her.

"I was not holding up anyone. They could do their work, if they wanted to" she replied.

"But by talking to them, you stopped them from concentrating on what they were doing. You liked to argue and did not accept responsibility for your behavior."

"I knew, I knew every teacher said that I did not accept what was not true. If I did not do my class work, it should not be anyone's concern, but mine. I would be happy, if you would leave me alone, and you did not pick on me."

She got up and moved to the back seat, and sat forcefully, dragged her chair put her head on the desk, pretending to be sleeping.

Alpha gave up the idea of keeping control of his class, as things got worst and worst. He also gave up the idea of keeping the job as well he was now looking forward to moving on which he thought was not only quite certain, but would be a relief for him.

The school administrators were now treating Alpha like a dump to vent their anger and frustration and made him felt that the job was not worth the insults, relegations, belittlement and open dislike of him by those in the office simply because he was a black substitute teacher who could be replaced at any time.

Mr. Humbla was now exercising more and more pressure on Alpha, treating him like an idiot the assistant principal could just push Alpha around and made him felt like an intern learning to teach. He had no one to complain to because he was black, the entire white teachers in the school did not like him and they would not talk to him. The administrators were like gods, anything they sent to the district office would be rubber stamped approval.

He came to Alpha's classroom twice a day each day of the week to check on everything Alpha was doing.

Why me all the time Alpha thought, there were scores of teachers in the building, mostly whites and a handful of others, but Mr. Humbla preferred to spend more time visiting my class to harass me which was quite unusual in normal circumstances.

This was one good example of how poor the system was maintained, putting more emphasis on misplaced priorities and the "who was who syndrome" as the driving force.

People knew that there were mountains of disciplinary problems in every school, very poor state results and some teachers were not teaching, but the lords of the manor turned a blind eye to these obvious problems and blamed the army of substitutes for polluting the schools.

All the serious problems that plagued the schools and the system were not important on the agenda of any discussion by the school officials. The most important thin was getting rid of those with an accent like alpha and blaming them for the ills of the system would be a hot topic on any agenda.

Every teacher in every school building in the whole district was doing his own thing and even the head of department would not come and asked you what you taught today or how far you were with the teaching schedule. No accountability to any one about anything except handing in your reports to guidance on time.

I was not the only substitute in the building but the others were white and so he did not border with them.

Alpha thought of reporting the issue to the teachers union, but he felt that since he was a substitute and black, the end result would be at his own disadvantage so he decided to endure the insults and relegation.

It was now worst than supervising a student teacher, and offering no help when students misbehaved. He found pleasure in treating a black man like a nutter and offered no suggestions in any way. Mr. Humbla could never had dreamt of treating any one of the white teachers in the building including white substitutes teachers who were less qualified and without teaching experience like the way he was treating Alpha.

He did everything to prove that a black teacher was worst than a below average white teacher. He was bullying Alpha like a subordinate under his care not realizing that Alpha was trained and more qualified than himself with all his official position, simply because he was white and carried the seal of authority and Alpha was a black African and just a substitute teascher.

He had told Alpha not to send any student outside the class, and none of Alpha's discipline referrals were acted upon. Students knew that Alpha could not do anything about their behavior in his classes since they knew that the assistant principal would not act on his referrals.

Jesus was so disruptive one afternoon, that he decided to call for an administrator, but no one showed up.

He wrote a discipline referral, which Jesus took from him by force, screwed it up and threw it over the window. Alpha was upset, but he controlled his anger he told Jesus to go and sit down, but he refused to sit down. Alpha made a second call for an administrator, but no one came. He took another discipline referral form to write up Jesus again. Jesus came up to him, looked at the discipline referral, with his name on it.

"Mr. Alpha did not waste your time writing me up. Mr. Humbla would not read it he said you wrote too many discipline referrals about students. He was going to put it in the garbage anyway" he went hack to his seat.

Alpha wrote the referral and handed it by hand to Mr. Humbla.

Next morning, Alpha saw Jesus passed by his room he was back in Alpha's fifth class with the same behavior

Alpha went to him to talk to follow him outside for a short conference. Alpha looked at Jesus with stern eyes

Jesus looked confused at first and then he said Mr. Alpha why did you blame me all the time for anything that happened in the class?" he said in a calm voice, every one in class acted up. Sometimes my mom did not give me my medicine, which I needed to take every morning before coming to school. I was sorry for my behavior, but sometimes I could not help it. It's all my mom's fault. But listen, Mr. Alpha, there were four boys in here who use drugs every day. If you checked in their book bags, you would find marijuana, or some other doping drugs. But please did not say I was the one that told you." he whispered into Alpha's ears.

"But did you yourself use these drugs?" Alpha asked, looking into his eyes.

Jesus went silent; bent his head down and then he nodded twice, and walked back into the classroom quickly. Alpha could see the guilt written on his face.

Alpha rushed back into the class to get the students who were screaming and shouting to be quiet.

He caught Hector throwing a textbook out of the window. "Why did you throw that book out of the window?" Alpha asked calmly.

"Who me? I did not throw a book out of the window" he replied in a loud angry and defiant voice.

"I saw you throwing the book, why didn't you accept your fault."

"I said I did not throw a book out" he was screaming, he took his book bag and left the room.

Alpha wrote a discipline referral for him. The period ended without any formal teaching.

It was the middle of the third period when Mrs. Zian the head of department, a white lady who had been in the school for many years came in. She came in with a textbook that had been ruined. "Excuse me, this was one of your text books wasn't it?" She flipped the pages over. "This book had been ruined. Mr. Tairo picked it from outside apparently thrown out by one of your students. This was not acceptable, you realized that. Each of these books cost $85, and to have it in this condition without a culprit was not good." she said looking into Alpha's eyes.

"I caught one student throwing a book out of the window. I wrote him for it, but I had no idea what they did to the student."

"If the student denied that he did not throw the book out, what did you do?" she asked.

"But I saw him, I questioned him about it, but he was very rude and insolent to me. So who did you believe the student or me who saw him?"

"It was not a case of for or against. My point was it was your responsibility to preserve these books It cost a lot of money to replace a whole set of text books." You could see the fury and anger on her face. She was breathing heavily.

This was really unfair, to police these students at the same time to teach them, he thought. She never came into that room when a white lady was substituting in the room. She never came in to check the books before Alpha came in and she never came into the room when Alpha came to substitute after the previous substitute left. She was convinced that it was Alpha who let the students ruined all the books in the room because he was black and apparently inefficient and could not control the students.

Five substitutes all white had walked out from the same room for the same discipline problems. But Alpha the black sheep the sixth substitute in the same room in one single school year was the one every one took notice of as the most inefficient substitute in the building that could not control his classes.

"It was a fact that teaching job was more of police work, because you spend more time on discipline than teaching nearly everyday. You had to keep control of these students you know. We knew that some of them were very difficult, but it was your responsibility. But remember, they were just kids, you had to discipline them in your classroom. Those who did not behave and obeyed the rules, you knew what to do with them."

She walked out of the room with angry steps.

Alpha was lost for words. "I came in the middle of a situation, I did not create, some teachers had come and failed to get into grips with this situation and had walked away. This was a classroom where no permanent teacher had been for three year." He stamped his foot "Substitutes were not taken seriously by teachers, administrators and even students. They saw us substitutes as untrained and inexperienced and just baby sitters.

The system used us as stop gap, teachers in schools did not trust us the substitutes. The students saw us as baby seaters. Students in any class saw the substitute not a real teacher, and the day as free day. Students did not take substitutes seriously, because they felt that the substitute knew nothing about the subject, and did not know their names. So a substitute represented a free day for the students. Since teachers often went into classrooms of absent colleagues one at a time, the day they see a new face in class. "Were you a teacher or a substitute?" they would ask one after another.

"A substitute" Alpha would answer "Oh easy, a free day" One student would run out to inform the rest of the class.

"We have a substitute today" The news would echo down the corridor "Free period," they would be shouting, as they came in.

Alpha got to know that if he said "I was a teacher, but I was substituting today the students would be more respectful of him. The situation would change very little. A new face in class would always represent a substitute and free day for the class. Free in the students views include free from being written up for detention or focus room. Free from class work because the substitute did not give grades or made students did work if they did not want to do, Free from all restrictions imposed by regular class teacher. A Substitute calling the office for help confirmed to the administration the accepted position that Substitutes did not do a good job. When it was necessary to call for help, the administrator sent out would usually expect you to have memorized the names of all the students in the class and their faces. He or she would want you to give the name of the student instanta.

They always expected you to be more effective than the regular teacher and to keep the students under iron hand discipline. Discipline referrals written by regular teachers would always receive immediate action, but those written by substitutes were not given due attention. The students knew that the substitute teachers did not know their names and so they would play all types of tricks on you.

CHAPTER ELEVEN

EARLY NEXT WEDNESDAY MORNING, Alpha was called out and told to go to the South River Middle school for three days. He got to school early, signed on and was handed the homeroom folder room 901. Alpha looked at the folder briefly first then a second look when he stopped and he was breathing fast he thought his heart was going to stop beating. "Hi Alpha one of the teachers said to him smiling he returned the smile. He walked out of the office into the corridor. He saw those old familiar faces, some smiling, others looked indifferently. "Here I go again" he told himself. "Well, it was only three days" he assured himself. He received mixed reception, as he walked to his room. Some students came forward to shake his hand. "Oh my God, Mr Alpha was here again." shouted some students. "Were you going to be our teacher for ever?" some students asked as he opened the door and entered the room. "We had sent one teacher packing, and you had come back into this room yet again."

Alpha looked round the room, all familiar faces of students he had last year in the seventh grade, with the exception of a few faces. Alpha knew what to expect. "These were the students I had last year, and so he expected the assignment to be very difficult.

The Homeroom ended, and in came the first period with the inclusion teacher Mrs. Hubert walked into the room. The room was noisy he could hardly get the students to settle down.

"Let us be quiet, the room was too noisy" shouted Mrs. Hubert the inclusion teacher. "I tell you what, when Mr. Bee was here, these students were quiet" she said quietly to Alpha.

But the teacher left because he had enough before Alpha came in. The noise went on and Alpha stood, and waited for them to be quiet before introducing the lesson. "Listen guys, you were not behaving like this when Mr. Bee was here" she repeated to the students in vain

This was the attitude of white teacher assistants who tried to tell Alpha indirectly that the classes were better when a white teacher was there. But Alpha knew that several other substitutes all white had walked away from this room because of the behavior of these students. Alpha found the room in disorder because the last teacher left in a hurry but Mrs. Hubert was giving the impression that the white substitute teacher who was there before Alpha had a better control and cooperation from the students. Alpha did not want to put her in a bad spot since she was white and all the administrators were white and they would listen to her and not to Alpha and so he let sleeping dogs to lie.

Alpha was busy writing on the board when a paper ball hit Mrs. Hubert on the back of her head. Alpha turned round just in time to see the paper flying to her head. "Kevin" Alpha shouted. The whole class burst out laughing.

"Its not funny." he roared in an angry voice. "Throwing missals at teachers was not funny" he went on.

"It's not a missal, just a piece of paper" said Gary laughing. "You could not and should not throw anything at a teacher period" he said in a stern voice.

"She was not a teacher, but an assistant" Jason said.

"She was a teacher we would write you up for this." Alpha told them. Mrs. Hubert was showing an indifferent attitude towards the incident.

The class ended as it begun. Less than half the lesson was covered.

Each day was not different from the previous day. The assistant principal Mr. Taito came in the third period.

"Listen guys, I was getting a lot of reports from other teachers about this room. This man was a substitute, and he was trying to teach you something, and you were not cooperating with him. He was better than other substitutes who come in and sat down reading their newspaper all day. No one was responsible for this situation. It was not my fault, it was not his fault," pointing to Alpha, and certainly not your fault the teacher who was here decided to resign and went away. We brought this man who was qualified, and teaching you which was better than bringing in daily substitutes who spend the day doing nothing. If you did not cooperate with him and failed you would have yourselves to blame. If I got any discipline referrals from this man, you would go home for three days" he left after receiving a message on the intercom.

"Why didn't you bring a white substitute teacher" one student shouted to him as he walked out of the door. Alpha felt funny. "That was a stupid question" said Mrs. Hubert. "It was not stupid, he had a point" replied Josue at the back. Some students mumbled statements which Alpha did not hear, followed by laughers.

It was the middle of the week in the afternoon the bell just rang for the end of the fifth period. Mrs. Hubert took her parcel of papers walked towards the door, then stopped. Mr. Alpha may be these students were refusing to do work because they felt that it was not challenging enough. You may not realize that, but some of these students were very smart" She walked out of the door in a hurry.

Alpha was rearranging the desks and picking up hand outs left on the desks. Alpha was baffled by Mrs. Hubert's statement "how could she say that, when all the students in the class were IEP students of various categories of behaviors and a range of intellectual deficiencies.

Some were too lazy to even write their names on the lined paper given out to do the work. Some barely completed one sentence in one hour after several prompts. Alpha found out that the previous teacher was white, and as usual students had all the respect for white teachers and tended to behave more appropriately towards them but the students' general behavior was bad and the administrators were of no help and sometimes it was a waste of time trying to correct a situation.

It was the general attitude that being a white teacher was acceptable since all the administrators were white and had respect for the white substitute teachers and listened to their complaints about student behavior and acted on those complaints. But that was the opposite with black substitutes like Alpha.

Teachers were not supposed to be black and so the students did not take black substitutes teachers seriously. They knew that the administrators did not respect them and listened to them why should they the students respect these black teachers.

Alpha remembered when a student said to him a black teacher wow. What was he doing here? I did not want a black teacher in my classroom. I would not listen to him no way I hated black teachers.

Two weeks past the situation did not get better the same students with the same behavior problems each day. "Writing up these students each day did not make any sense." he told himself. He knew that the more referrals he wrote the more convinced the administrators were that he was not doing his job effectively. The school administration was not interested in what the teacher was teaching, they were concerned only about the teachers effectiveness in terms of classroom management. As long as there were no referrals and no calls for help that was the right man for the job even if you did not teach anything at all.

But managing students with various behavior and learning problems was an up hill task, especially now that class detention had been reduced from fifteen minutes to five minutes after school, because the students had to catch their buses to go home, and there were no extra buses provided.

The students knew that you could not keep them for more than five minutes after school and so the after school detention had lost its meaning and purpose.

One morning Alpha was in the office to sign in and took his homeroom folder he met Mr. Sosada in the office. "Were you here again?" he asked Alpha in a surprised voice. "Yes, I was here in the same room, with the same students" he replied.

"Wow" he exclaimed. "And you were standing for it? That was punishment for you. I would never go back into that room for any reason even for a day" he told Alpha. "You were the only one who could withstand the behavior of those students. Good luck" he said and walked away. He was a white substitute teacher and he could speak his mind and the administrators and everyone else along the chain of command would listen to him and would respect his views.

But Alpha had no voice and no one would listen to him or bordered with his referrals. And certainly no one would accept any statement from him since no one wanted to say a word to him including the school administrators and those in the head office down town.

It was the end of the fourth period a very difficult lesson. Alpha was cleaning the board, when Mrs. Hubert said "I think the lesson was not challenging enough for the students that was why they were all restless." She walked out quickly before Alpha could say a word. "How could this white bitch said that when the other groups with normal students were complaining that the work was too hard and too much for one lesson.

She had told me before that the more work he gave them, the more they were occupied and the less they would misbehave and he collected all the work sheets left on the desks. There were only four completed sheets out of twenty two. "This was the fourth time she was criticizing the work, even though she did all the work for the inclusion students and had them just copy in their handwriting and she expected me to give them straight "A" grades" he thought.

"Mr Alpha these students needed top grades for their work, didn't they? She would ask. She gave her own grades to these students which she submitted to the guidance office for the inclusion students and those grades were accepted. No one cautioned her grades since she was white and Alpha's grades for the same students did not count, an element of weakness in the system and its administration and evidence of the disparity between grades and students ability.

Alpha found the practice quite distasteful, but from the vibes he got from the team members, he had to go along with the other teachers.

One Tuesday morning, it was the end of the third period. The assistant principal came to talk to the students about their behavior. Mrs. Hubert had her folder under her left armpit. The principal walked out, closed the door behind him. All the students left."Mr. Alpha, you may want to cover that graffiti on the display board. If the principal came in here and saw that, she would crucify you alive. She would have fits, "she walked out quickly before Alpha could open his mouth. Alpha was going to reply but had no time.

"The principal had been in the classroom four times to see how Alpha was doing she had patted Alpha's shoulder once when she came in" he told himself.

Nothing got better, each morning as Alpha came to his room which was next to the assistant principal's office, he would hear the assistant principal bargaining with some of the students." were you going to be good today? No play up, you promise" he would tell the student.

One afternoon, Alpha had a free period. He was quietly reading his news paper. He went to the bathroom, and found Edison sitting on the chair outside Ms Then's room. He came back into his room and continued reading the newspaper.

All of a sudden, a chair wagged at his door, smashing the glass. He ran out side quickly, and saw a boy with a yellow long T shirt disappearing from the end of the corridor. He called the office. The senior assistant principal came with the police posted in the school.

They inspected the window. "What happened?" asked the police.

"I did not know who did it, but Edison was sitting on this chair outside Ms Then's room moments ago. Then, I saw a boy in long yellow T shirt disappearing in that corner." Alpha told them.

The assistant principal radioed to the second floor, and a boy matching the description was intercepted.

Ms. Then came out of her room and said that Edison did it. "He was too bad in class, and I told him to sit on this chair outside the room.

Edison was brought up, but he denied that he did it. "I refused to sit on that chair" he told the administrator and the police.

Ms. Then insisted that he threw the chair of the glass door. The assistant principal and the police left. The boy Alpha saw disappearing admitted that he wagged the chair on the door.

The team members were very hostile to Alpha after that incident the only male in the team. The team leader who was the private confidant of the principal did not like Alpha either and the senior assistant principal who was also black African- American. She made open statements in their team meetings about her dislike of the assistant principal.

The team members hardly spoke to Alpha except if they had to, and they blamed him for every disciplinary problem within the team. Students run up and down the corridors all the time. They blamed Alpha for letting out students from his room who went out and cause problems for other teachers. A no pass policy was arranged within the team in their weekly meeting.

Students complained to the assistant principal for not letting them out to go to the bathroom the assistant principal then told Alpha to let students go to the bathroom if they wanted to.

But the teachers in the team pointed a finger at him for relaxing the team's no pass policy. He told them the assistant principal told him to let students went to the bathroom, but they still blamed him for letting students out of his room against the team's policy. He was the black scape goat.

During lunch time the following day one student threw an apple at Mrs. wilder's head. Alpha was blamed for not giving the name of the boy who threw the apple, even though he was not present at the scene he only knew about it from other students.

He was blamed for the incident because they alleged that one of his students threw the apple and that he knew who did it

His students were just moving down into the cafeteria and they would not have handled apples besides he was with them in the corridor on their way into the cafeteria. He could have seen who threw the apple. But where would students on their way to the cafeteria obtained apples found only in the cafeteria. But he was the black sheep and he was the culprit and he carried the blame squarely.

The general school attendance was falling fast as more and more students were absent from school each day.

But they decided to blame Alpha for marking absent students who were in the building but not in his homeroom. The assistant principal told Alpha to mark present all students present in the building. "But how would I know that a student was present if they did not come into the homeroom.

It was all like a vendetta and a real joke because one teacher alone among over sixty teachers would hardly affect adversely the over all attendance of six hundred students with four or five absences day. It was obvious to every one in the school that children could come to school up to three hours late and they still marked these students present and sometimes without any deterrent like detention.

The matter went to the principal through the team leader who served as private secretary to the principal.

The principal expressed concern that the school attendance roll was falling down too fast, because students in the building were marked absent in the attendance register each day.

"He was guilty of that" shouted Mrs. Thimoro pointing her finger at Alpha. Alpha discovered that his attendance folder was being inspected by the other teachers who took it from students by force before it went down to guidance office every day.

One lunch period, students were rushing to lunch, and an apple was thrown at Mrs. Wilder again from the crowd of students who were rushing in all directions, which hit her at the back of the head. She did not know who threw the apple Alpha was not there at the time.

But Alpha was in the office signing out for break he overheard Mrs. Wilder telling the secretary that she was going home. She had a headache, that one of Alpha's students hit her with an apple. The corridor was full of students from all classrooms, those from the cafeteria and the students going down to the cafeteria. Alpha's students were just going to the cafeteria at the time and they would not have had applies to throw around. But Alpha always carried the garbage can in the school for any incident whether he was near there or not. His name was in the fore front for any blame to be apportioned to individual teachers in the school.

It was early afternoon one Thursday, Alpha had a rough day, with a near fight in his second period, and books were thrown out of the window by Jesus and Shawn. These were students Alpha could write up each day, but it did not make sense, because they spent most of their time in Focus room anyway. But their behavior never changed. Alpha's voice grew very faint by the end of the day.

He went to the office to deposit discipline referrals when he overheard the assistant principal Mr Taito who was a navy office before becoming assistant principal told the office staff. "I spent one year in Vietnam in the war front, expecting to die at any moment. But I enjoyed it more than what I was doing in this building. We had a fighting school today one fight after another and this was not what I signed in for. I have been here from seven in the morning till seven in the evening. I never thought things would go as bad as they were going and they seemed to get worst each day.

If I tripped and fell please call an ambulance for me, because I did not know how long my health would hold up and my body would go on under these circumstances." he said in a low voice. The Principal came in and he walked away quickly through the side door to the corridor.

The next day Alpha stayed in his room rearranging the desks. He walked downstairs he witnessed a female student mouthing the assistant principal. Alpha was ashamed of himself what he heard from the mouth of the student who was talking to the assistant principal like she was talking to an infant child. Every one stood, covering their mouths with surprised and disgust, not believing what they heard from a female student.

The team meetings Alpha attended each week were all about discipline. "I did not know, but we have never had such a bad group of students in all my thirteen years in this school" said Mrs. Thimoro.

The idea of shifting students around came up, suggestions on who to move around was conscientious, but no action was taken in the end, and the discipline in the team never got better.

It was lunch time Alpha was coming back into his room when the assistant principal Mr. Taito stopped him "You knew what, you were about to get a write up, and you would be barred from coming back into the building. You needed to get your classes under control. Every teacher in your team was complaining about you. If we decided against you, you might never come back into this building" he walked away quickly down the corridor.

Alpha knew that he had write ups that have been kept in his file for more than four years even though the Union contract stated that no negative write ups should be kept in a teacher's file for more than one calendar year. They had used these write ups to stop him from being given a permanent job and complaining would be like starting a war with the District that would certainly end his career with the district. But the union contract applied only to those

in the good books of the administrators and those in the category of special teachers who were protected not only the union laws but nepotism, ethnicity, color coding and more invisible considerations. Alpha did not belong in any of the categories and so he was an invisible man in the ocean of discriminatory practices under the large umbrella of equal opportunities.

Alpha decided to make a move because another write up would be total destruction of his career. He went to see the Director of human resources. After a few trials he had the opportunity to talk to him face to face and he asked that he be moved to another position in another school because he already had enough discrimination in the school he was assigned to. He explained the problems he was facing and how unhappy he was in his present position.

I see your problems, but consider the time of year and the interest of the students. You have been with them all this time, and to leave them now and move to another school would not be in their best interest. Talk to the Principal, and then come back to me" he told Alpha.

Alpha had a meeting with the principal one afternoon. She was accommodating and understanding. She denied that there was going to be a write up on him. "I have interviewed you, and knew that you knew what you were doing. But classroom management and the discipline in the school at the moment was not making things better for the teachers.

Each day I prayed that I go home in one piece." She rubbed her forehead, patted her hair.

Nest morning Alpha received a hearty welcome from the assistant principal, who hardly talked to him before for some time now.

"You were the right man for the job" he said in a deep voice. Things improved in the relationship with the administrators.

Each morning Mr Taito would ask Alpha if he would like to keep the students for detention for a few minutes until he came up after dispatching students into their buses.

"Yes, please" Alpha would reply. Alpha wanted to be in the good books of the assistant principal. One afternoon the fifteen minutes turned out to be fifty five. The other time he did not get home until five in the afternoon. "Alpha did not like doing it, but he had no alternative, because if he kept saying no, Mr. Taito would develop a negative attitude towards Alpha all over again.

"You were a good man" he would say as he cam in to take over. Alpha's room became the regular afternoon detention room.

The atmosphere between Alpha and the assistant principal changed for the better but not with the team teachers. They still regarded Alpha as an Alien and not a bona fide member of the group. Being a man and only man in the team made things worst in addition to being a black man with an accent.

One afternoon, it was planning time Alpha got to Mrs. Thimoro's room early and he was busy writing something in his diary when Mrs. Thimoro whispered to Ms Then. Alpha lifted his head and saw her talking to Ms Then in whispers.

That Alpha had been fire. The news spread like wild fire even though Alpha was a long term substitute and had been substituting over the years. Alpha was not worried about the news because all the principal could have done was to request the transfer of Alpha to another school and got another substitute into the school or filled the vacancy with one of the many substitutes going around or recommended some one to be hired by the school district. He was not a regular teacher to be fired by the principal and even regular teachers were employed and paid by the school district and not the individual schools

It was graduation time some students in Alpha's classes had proposed a class party in Alpha's room.

It was later agreed that the whole team be invited to the party. Each teacher was to bring some food or drink. Alpha said students had asked him to bring a party cake. The teachers wanted the school to pay for the food. Mrs. Thimoro promised to talk to her friend the principal if the principal would give them a check for the party.

Mrs. Hubert collected the receipt from Alpha for the cake, promising that the team teachers would share the bill equally. Alpha brought the cake, but it was never shared to the students. Nobody said anything to Alpha about the cake or the cost of the cake.

It was time to work out the final grades for the graduating students. In a team meeting the teachers were told that there were too many failures. The emphasis had been that most students should graduate, no matter what.

Each teacher should revise his or her grades and should allow more students pass.

Every week, a list of who would pass or fail was to be submitted to the principal for readjustment and revision downwards to increase the number of students graduating.

It was decided that all students should pass, including those destined for "Es" and "Fs". In the end all the students passed and graduated making the grades apparently irrelevant and a complete waste of time doing those grades after all.

Some of the students who did not obtained a passing grade in a single subject walked on the stage at graduation ceremony when in fact only those who passed with good grades should walk on the stage. But they all walked on the stage as a matter of convenience and received diplomas.

Alpha was surprised to see one inclusion student who the inclusion teacher did all the class work for and had a "C" in Alpha's grade book and computer print out walked on the stage as an honor student. One other inclusion student who had a computer print out with all "B+" grades had "C" and "C-" in Alpha's grade book.

Inclusion students normally had problems and so they had a teacher who went round with them to help them with their class work and home work. But these special education teachers gave these students top grades even thought they the teachers did all the work for these students spoon feeding them and making the class grades in general valueless and not reflecting ability in most cases a general problem in the system exemplified in state exam results.

Mrs. Hubert told Alpha to go to the office and protest about the grades. Alpha refused" saying "I was not going to stick my neck out on anything, because everybody knew that grade changes went on all the time. I did not want to be a scape goat in the last minute when everything else had gone wrong.

CHAPTER TWELVE

Mr. Alpha moved to the middle school in Garbon Street. Life was never better, the divide between blacks and whites was still distinct and clear cut.

The veteran teachers clearly did not like Alpha because of his color and accent. Each time he approach any one of them for help or even simply to talk to them, they will show a cold shoulder and walked away to avoid him.

The principal was a Blackman with a typical African accent. The assistant principal was a black American woman and quite strict and kids feared her more than the principal.

Teachers resented the authority of the principal but subtly. All negative talk about the principal was in whispers. Alpha got to know that the principal was teaching in the school the previous year. He was moved to another school in the Far East of Sarawali city and he was recalled to come back and head the school. The faculty was predominantly white and the idea of a black man heading the school did not go down well. Two teachers resigned and left the school in protest.

Alpha took the vacancy of one of these teachers. Students too resent the idea of a black man being principal. As the principal made announcements in the mornings, you could hear the resentments in your homeroom from students "oh here we go. Shut up and speak English, did not spit on the mike, he could not speak proper English."

In general if you spoke English with an accent other than American accent, where ever you went be it government, private, the police or any office or any institution, you were deemed not to speak good English. Students had often told Alpha in class to speak proper English.

Alpha had told students on several occasions that he attended five English Universities in Europe. "But you were not speaking good English? "You were not speaking English at all" another student would shout out. Speak English the students would tell Alpha in class many times.

Alpha had a rough year, because the students did not cooperate with him and he received no help from the other teachers. Veteran teachers expected Alpha too fail so that they would use that as an excuse to show that he was not competent as a black teacher.

The principal recommended Alpha for a promotion to fill in the vacant position, and he was eventually appointed as a regular teacher on probation.

In the second year another assistant principal came in who was more racist than the previous assistant principal. Mr. Provoh had a very negative attitude towards Alpha. Some students thought that his oriental attitude was not quite acceptable but being the man in charge of discipline was a forward runner in discipline matters in the school since discipline occupied more administrator and teacher time than teaching.

He was of the opinion that all school problems originated from Alpha's room, and so he visited Alpha's room many times a day. Each time there was a problem in the school, his first thought was that it originated from Alpha's room and so he would try to associate the problem with students in Alpha's room or those leaving his room.

Mr. Provoh found a soda drink spilled out side the corridor near Alpha's room one afternoon, where all the students coming from the cafeteria passed by, and he accused Alpha that his students did spill the soda drink. It turned out to be false because Alpha's students had not gone out for lunch yet, but being the only black sheep in the flock of whites he was an easy and soft target for any accusation.

Students were pulling the fire alarm at odd intervals and while the investigations were going on to find out who was pulling the alarm, the principal announced on the intercom that one teacher upstairs was letting out students who were pulling the alarms. Fingers were pointed at Alpha and it turned out that a boy in the sixth grade was actually pulling the alarms.

The boy confessed and the vindication of Alpha became obvious yet again accusing the black man without foundation but an easy target.

The scape goating of Alpha went on without mercy, and the party of humiliation for the African man with an accent went on without a break.

Alpha was becoming very uneasy with the harassment as Mr. Provoh visited his classroom many times each day, making negative comments each time and he told Alpha that he was going to put his name in his black list. Alpha decided to tell the Principal about the threat.

The principal assured Alpha that no body was going to put his name on a black list without his approval as head of the school.

Mr. Provoh would ignore Alpha on the corridors after that and he would not talk to Alpha any more. Mr. Provoh would not answer if Alpha said hi or good morning to him, he would pretend not to hear or simply just ignored Alpha.

Alpha was a black sheep in a sea of white environment. He never got help and he felt that there was a concerted effort to make him fail so that fingers could be pointed at him for poor classroom management. Students made racist remarks at him in class, he would write up the students, but no action from the assistant principal and even if he complained to other teachers no body seemed to pay attention or offered a solution.

If any of these teachers wrote a student, action would be taken immediately. Alpha had been told by students that he was wasting his time writing them up because the referral would be thrown into the dustbin.

It was one morning, when jasmine came to class in her usual defiant and rude manner. Alpha had written this girl many times for racist remarks, the principal was well aware of this problem, calling Alpha a black monkey, a black ass, uneducated because he did not speak good English and not fit to be a teacher since he could not speak English with an American accent.

She was very disrespectful of Alpha and openly defiant. She came to class in the usual defiant mod and ready to swear at Alpha if he dare talked to her or told her to behave or move to her assigned seat. The assistant principal was aware of this problem but choose to ignore it. She would talk while Alpha explained the lesson to the class all the time and ignoring the teachers orders.

When Mr. Alpha told her to be quiet she would flair up and she would say all nasty words to the teacher. Sometimes sending her out was the only solution. She would use any words that came into her head on the teacher.

It was despicable to get nasty words from a little girl who could be a grand daughter of Alpha. Mr. Alpha decided not to write up the student because the assistant principal would not read his referrals and so the matter would be dead before he left the office. Mr. Provoh would accept a student's explanations of a situation from Alpha's room and he would ignore Alpha's explanations.

This was yet again the disadvantage of being black in a white racist society where color syndrome had turned most people into open racist individuals not only on schools, but in stores, malls, offices and on the streets.